HEROES
ALSO
DIE

HEROES ALSO DIE

MICHAEL GELLER

ST. MARTIN'S PRESS
NEW YORK

Library of Congress Cataloging-in-Publication Data

Geller, Michael R.
  Heroes also die.

  "A Thomas Dunne book."
  I. Title.
PS3557.E3793H47   1988   813'.54   87-28639
ISBN 0-312-01441-4

First Edition
`10 9 8 7 6 5 4 3 2 1

Grateful acknowledgment is made to Kenneth Siegelman for permission to use his poem "The Stakeout."

THE STAKEOUT

My footsteps
Echo in the alleyway.
Pinching toes
Numb
Like pitch nighttime.
Shoe taps
Deafen in stampede—
Just a blur
Around the corner.

Atop the paint-chipped
      porch,
Canopied elm eyes
Drop a burden
Of suspicion
Like the squeaking slats,
Which now
Stop dead.

In the empty space
Between the guilty look
Of knowing
I have seen
Him blink
Flush-faced alarm,
And my footsteps
Blindly thundering
Down the alleyway.

       —Kenneth Siegelman
       1987

HEROES
ALSO
DIE

. . . .

Take a picture of his *what*?"

"Will you pipe down, Benny."

People at the other tables were turning around.

"A lot of guys told me that you were a sicko, Slots, but I always said no. I mean, you got your funny ways, but I always thought—"

"It's not what you think, Benny. It's for a case."

"Sure!" He looked at me over the top of his bi-focals. "You should be ashamed of yourself." He shook his head.

I had just wined and dined Benny at his favorite restaurant, The Roumanian Gourmet, where he had polished off a loaf of black bread and a half gallon of borscht. His shirt, an Omar the Tent Maker original, looked ready to burst.

"Don't tell me you haven't done this kind of thing before, Benny. I happen to know that you're on the payroll of three of the scummiest tabloids around."

"I deny that!" he said indignantly.

Benny worked in the medical examiner's office.

Tomorrow they would have Pinto's body released and ready for viewing. If I didn't want to go and dig up his grave, I had to talk Benny into taking the picture for me.

"Slots, do you know why I've been affiliated with the coroner's office for over twenty years? Do you know why I am the most trusted employee and most well-respected technician on the medical examiner's staff?"

"Benny, all—"

"The reason, Slots, is that I take pride in my job. I believe in the sanctity of death. I feel that we are all diminished by the passing of one. 'No man is an island,' my friend. 'Do not ask for whom the bell tolls, it tolls for thee.'"

"Are you going to get me a picture of his ass or not?"

"Not."

"Fine. Then I tell my client that you turned down the three hundred and that's that."

"Three hundred, you say?"

"Three hundred."

"Would you like color or black-and-white? I could use a Polaroid, but you'd get a better shot with a thirty-five millimeter."

"I need the left cheek. He's supposed to have a strawberry mole."

"How much are you getting out of this, Slots?"

I thought about the dinner I'd just had with him. "Not enough, Benny, not enough."

"Slots"—he leaned over and put his hand to his mouth—"what can I get if I turn him over and take another shot?"

"Please, Benny. Just the strawberry."

"Hey, don't get so high and mighty. You're the guy that wants the picture. You're the one who's paying for it."

                    *   *   *

I wasn't paying for it, but that wasn't Benny's business. My clients were two girls in their late teens named Jan and Fran. Fran was the one with blue eyes and brown hair, and Jan was the one with brown eyes and blue hair. Their bodies in halter tops and tight shorts were enough to make you forget about their Bride of Frankenstein hairstyles and the two safety pins stuck in their respective ears.

It took a little while for me to understand what they were saying. I keep a box of tissues on my desk and they had to have gone through half with grief-driven weeping and sniffling. What I finally got figured out between the tears, the "y'knows," and the "mans" was that they were the national copresidents of the Ned Pinto Fan Club. They couldn't believe that their idol was dead. They were convinced that it was a plot of some kind engineered by the Russians, or that Pinto had had a disfiguring accident and was really in hiding until he could have plastic surgery.

"We don't care how he looks. We love him no matter what," Jan told me tearfully.

"We just want him back," Fran pleaded.

I spent a quarter of an hour trying to convince them that Pinto was really dead. I went over the facts as presented by every TV station, newspaper, magazine, radio newscast, and smoke signal.

Pinto had escaped death twice, once at his Malibu home and once in his hotel, the Hyatt in New York. The third try was the charm: he was gunned down in his limousine by a man riding a bicycle through the traffic-choked streets. The man, who made a clean getaway but was shortly thereafter captured, was a Vietnam vet named Thomas Noolan, "Crazy Tommy" to those who knew him well. Tommy resented all the publicity around Pinto's Rally for

3

America; he felt that Pinto was getting all the fame and glory that rightfully should go to the vets. So he decided to correct the situation and strike a blow for his buddies by gunning the beloved actor down. Pinto, who strove above all to protect his "Iron Man" image, had spurned police protection, despite the two prior near misses.

Ned Pinto was shot at close range by a Browning automatic Noolan purchased in the Automat after he arrived from California. Ballistics had matched up the rifle found in Noolan's L.A. apartment to the first attempt on Pinto's life. Two police officers at the Hyatt identified Noolan as the man posing as a busboy who tried to get into Pinto's room, and who subsequently gunned down Officer J. J. Mitchell.

I rattled off all the facts in a logical, factual, and I thought convincing style. The two girls took it all in and stared vacantly at me. When I was finished, Jan wanted to know if I would take the case.

"Didn't you understand what I was telling you?" I asked.

"Yes," Fran said, "but we don't believe it."

"Nobody could possibly kill the Iron Man," Jan said.

For years we have been told that TV and movies can addle our brains and turn them into mush. The two girls sitting in my office and dabbing at their eyes were living proof that this is so.

"What would it take to convince you?" I finally asked in exasperation. "The body will be on display and you can see for yourselves that he's dead."

"A double," Fran said.

Jan nodded in agreement.

"Right! I should have thought of that," I said.

"Look Mr. Resnick, we know that you're expensive, but we're willing to pay you to help us prove that he's still alive. We have five thousand dollars," Fran said.

Jan started tossing bundles of money from her pocketbook onto my desk.

"Where did you get that kind of money?"

"It's from the members of the club. We were supposed to buy tickets for the Rally for America concert. We have two hundred members at twenty-five dollars a ticket. That's five thousand, right?"

"If not, it's close enough," I said.

"This means a lot to us, Mr. Resnick. We can't go home and face the members if we don't try to get to the bottom of what happened."

"But girls, I'm sorry; we already know what happened."

They shook their heads.

It finally dawned on me that to them, Ned Pinto was the equivalent of Kennedy, King, and Gandhi. In spite of their looks and lack of sophistication, the pain they were feeling was quite real. It also dawned on me that if I didn't accept the case, they would march out the door and find someone who would gladly take their money and go through the motions.

"If I could prove to you that Pinto actually was murdered, would you accept it and go home? By the way, where is home?" I asked.

"Shreveport," Fran said. "If you could prove it to our satisfaction."

"Do you have any idea how I could do that?"

"You're the detective," Jan said.

"Right!" I sighed.

Jan tapped Fran on the shoulder and the two of them went into a private huddle.

"There is a way," Fran said. "Ned has a strawberry mole on his left bun. If we could see that, we'd know."

"Did you read that someplace? Are you sure that's accurate?"

"We didn't read that; we knew Ned."

I tried to be delicate. "When you say you *knew*

him, the both of you, you are implying that you knew him in the biblical sense of the word?"

"No, we mean that we screwed him all day when he got here from California," Fran said.

"Yeah, and we remember the mole because he made us kiss it for luck," Jan offered.

I nodded. "Foolish of me not to think of that."

f there had been such a category in my high school yearbook as Least Likely to be Photographing a Deceased Movie Star's Tush, I would have won it with ease. My father, Jacob Resnick, a cantor of reknown on the East Side synagogue circuit, and my mother, Bridget Kelly, of the Fighting Kellys of Fourth Street, didn't raise their son Mickey to engage in such frivolous pursuits.

According to them, I was destined to break out of the bounds of Hell's Kitchen and do great things. The odds against it were pretty high: of the ten guys who made up the neighborhood crew, six had served time at Rikers before they graduated high school. Two of the six wound up on death row after an armed stickup went sour.

The thing that saved me was baseball. My school team went on to become city champs, and I raised a few admiring eyebrows with a hefty .417 batting average. I was offered a choice of going to Arizona State on a baseball scholarship or signing with the Mobile Gamers, the Detroit Tigers' affiliated farm club. The former offered an education, the latter a twenty-five-thousand-dollar bonus.

I knew that if I accepted the scholarship no major league club could legally approach me until at least three years from the date of entrance into the school. If baseball was to be my life, I decided, I didn't want school to interfere. On the Gamers, I would be playing, eating, and sleeping baseball with professionals, some of whom had already been to the big leagues. I took the money.

On August fifteenth, in my first year of professional ball, I was leading the league in hits, bases on balls, and runs scored. I was third in the Southern League in batting average, and I was fielding my shortstop position better than adequately.

On one particular occasion, after going five for five against three different pitchers and winning the game with a bloop down the left-field line, the opposing manager was interviewed in the Durham *Post*:

> I have a lot of respect for the Gamers' young shortstop, Resnick. There's no way to defend against him. If we guard the lines, he goes up the middle. If we bring the infield in, he goes over our heads. We play deep, and he bunts us to death. No matter what we do, he finds the slots.

The name "Slots" caught on with my teammates and was eventually picked up by the papers and the radio broadcasting teams. I didn't mind it, because it was easy for people to remember, and my whole reason for playing in Mobile was to get the major league clubs to take notice. A scout from the Tigers had assured me that I would be invited to the big club's spring training facility in Sarasota in March.

On August sixteenth, I was in an Atlanta hospital with a broken ankle suffered when an overzealous base runner upended me trying to break up a double play. When the cast came off, I'd be as good as new they assured me.

I wasn't. The speed and range in the field were gone, and more important, that sweet, natural swing became a memory. Everybody was sorry. It was a rough break. . . . If there was anything they could do. . . . If I would work on getting the swing back . . .

There I was, washed up at nineteen.

I became a cop. My father didn't like it, but eventually he got used to the idea. My mother's family was delighted; my grandfather was a retired detective, and two of my uncles were on the force.

This time the breaks were good. I was in the right place at the right time, and I made a couple of important collars. A friend from the old neighborhood gave me a tip about the Morgan Trust holdup and I broke the case. A year later I was able to track down the shipment of dynamite that had been used to blow up the steps of the federal courthouse on Foley Square. That led me to a warehouse on West Street where I nabbed FALN fugitive Luis Reyes. I was getting press, and I was being noticed. Things were really rolling.

I was living with a woman who was pushing me into marriage. Did I love her? I didn't know. We were comfortable together, and we were drifting into matrimony. It was all Harriet would talk about, and I was going to do it to please her. I was thirty, my future was solid, and although I wasn't sure about Harriet, maybe that would be okay, too.

Once or twice a day for about a week I was experiencing nausea. "Morning sickness" the guys in the precinct decided. I laughed, too, but had it checked out with my doctor. He sent me to a specialist for X-rays, who then called me in and offered me a cigarette. You know you're in trouble when your doctor offers you a smoke.

9

He didn't believe in coddling patients, he said. The X-rays showed an inoperable mass on my liver. I had a month, two or three at the outside. He was sorry. Send in the next patient, please.

I locked myself in a hot-sheet motel in Queens and stayed drunk for three days. I thought about all the things I would have done differently if only I had another chance. Out of sheer boredom, I called in and found that Dr. Bieng's office had been trying to reach me. It was urgent that I contact him.

I drove over in a semistupor and was ushered right in to the apologetic doctor.

There had been a terrible mistake, he explained. The girl had just brought him the wrong tray. He fired her, of course. No, there's nothing wrong with you, Mr. Resnick. Probably a virus or something. He was so sorry, but those things happened occasionally. Thanks for being so understanding. Send in the next patient, please.

I took out my gun and put it squarely between his eyes. "In thirty seconds I'm going to blow your brains out," I told him.

He thought I was kidding at first, but then he looked in my eyes and knew I wasn't.

He pleaded for his life. He told me it wasn't his fault. He offered me money. At the end of the thirty seconds, I forced myself to put the gun away and leave his office.

I changed. I started to spend my bonus money, which up to now had been gathering interest in a savings account. I bought clothes, jewelry, put a down payment on a new car. I started to live for myself.

Harriet didn't like it. She liked the old me: conservative, with both feet on the ground. In a little while, she moved out. I later discovered that it was a ploy to make me see how much I would miss her. It didn't work. I found myself free, emancipated. I was living!

1 0

There was some flack on the job. I wasn't concerned about the tons of forms, the chain of command, the office politics necessary to get ahead. I spent my time trying to find the bad guys, because I enjoyed the challenge of it, and because I was good at it. I may have stepped on a lot of brass toes, but the bottom line was that I got the job done.

I was Slots the Maniac, until the time I busted Jake Grogan, the Sutton Place Strangler. Then I became known as Chief of Detectives Mickey "Slots" Resnick.

The mayoral election saw the retirement of the police commissioner. There was talk at Police Plaza—where when someone sneezes on the roof, someone else says "God bless you" in the basement—that I was being considered for the job. The wags were wrong this time.

Orlando Vargas was appointed from outside the ranks. Vargas had done a good job as a federal prison director and he was handed the commissioner's job as a payoff to Bronx Councilman Ed Rosario. Rosario had delivered the Latino vote for the mayor-elect and he wanted to show his constituents that he wielded power: enter Vargas.

My first meeting with the new commissioner was my last. He told me that he believed in strict discipline. It was how he ran his outfit in the marines, and it was how he ran the prisons. I was an example: my dress, my clothes, my off-hour actions. He didn't like my flash, my lax attitude with the men. He talked until I told him where he could shove his job and walked out.

Exit Resnick.

I got offers from other towns and big cities, but I was a New York guy. Private security firms wanted me to direct their operations, but I just couldn't make the transition from catching murderers and bombers to stopping shoplifting in the A&P.

Enter Slots Resnick, private investigator.

. . . .

I called the girls back to my office and showed them Benny's photo exhibition. There were three shots and three different angles of the heart-shaped mole. The kids looked at each other and started the waterworks again.

After a while, I gave them back the five grand they had left with me, minus Benny's three hundred and another two fifty for my time. I should have figured they would want the pictures; something to share with the other members of the club back in Shreveport. I politely turned them down.

Out came the money again and they were dumping it on my desk. Forty-four fifty for the three shots!

Money has never been one of my strong suits. I can make it okay, but not fast enough to keep pace with my spending. At that moment, the four grand and change looked appetizing. I was a month late on my Porsche payment and the finance company's letters had switched from polite concern to threats. It was a 928, a candy-apple red job with SLOTS on the vanity plate. I wasn't giving that baby up without a fight.

My other big expense was the bottom floor of the Thirty-third Street brownstone that housed my offices. The three-room, fully furnished suite ate up my police department pension check. It was made more affordable by the fact that I slept on the pullout convertible in the waiting room.

I eyed the money for a moment and then pushed it back across the desk. I did have some standards. Cashing in on Pinto's death didn't appeal to me. I also owed it to Benny to be sure the pictures were destroyed.

The girls were persistent.

"Look, do you think that's how Ned Pinto would want to be remembered?" I asked them. "Don't we owe his memory something more than this?" I held up the pictures.

"I guess you're right," Fran said.

"He was so cute," Jan offered tearfully.

I ushered them out, passing platitudes and wearing my funeral director demeanor.

I took the pictures, put them in an ashtray, and torched them with my Zippo. That was the bottom line on Ned Pinto, so to speak.

Sherry called and canceled out on our date to see the Mets against the Cardinals at Shea. She was a broker—pardon me, a financial consultant—for one of the big firms on Wall Street. She told me that volume on the market had gone through the roof and she was going to be stuck doing paperwork till at least 9:30 P.M.

I told her not to worry and that I'd meet her for coffee after work.

"You buying?" she asked me.

My financial status was a priority of Sherry's.

"I think I can handle it. No danish, though."

"Knowing you, you might not be kidding," she shot back.

*   *   *

I've got a big bay window that looks out on the quiet tree-lined street. Down the block there is an elementary school and a thirty-story condo that sits like a giant gatepost on the corner.

Parking is a bitch. There's a garage available for two hundred a month. I pass. I could take my chances and park under the East River Drive and take a bus back to the office. I'll pass again. The only other solution is to ignore the alternate-side-of-the-street signs, pay the tickets, and hope they don't move the tow trucks back south of Thirty-fourth Street.

I thought I was going to get another ticket when I saw the sector car pull up in front of my brownstone. Morris Ackerman stepped out. Each city department has a mayoral aide who acts as a liaison between it and City Hall. The police department had Morris Ackerman. We had a long history of bad blood between us; Ackerman always complained that the mayor never got any publicity when there was a big collar.

"Couldn't you mention that it was the *mayor* who put extra detectives on the case?" "Why didn't you tell the papers that the *mayor* suggested that avenue of action?" "Did you tell the reporters that the *mayor* pushed the feds into coughing up the funding that helped you crack the case?"

I had this bad habit: I dished out credit to the guys in the field who really sweated their tails. That didn't make me popular with Ackerman. I couldn't prove it, but I was pretty sure that my pal Morris was the one who set Vargas against me.

"Very impressive, Slots," he said, looking around and taking the chair across from my desk. "A place like this has got to cost you."

"I get by."

"Sure you do. Well, how do you like retirement?"

"It's a little slice of heaven. What's on your mind,

Morris? I've got things to do, so if you're not going to offer me a fee, I've got to get back to the paying customers."

"Mm-hm." Morris pulled his pipe and a pouch of Sail out of the inside pocket of his sports jacket. He made a big production out of filling the pipe and getting it started. There're two kinds of people I can never seem to get along with: the first kind is the guys who have Playboy decals on their car windows; the second kind is pipe smokers. To paraphrase Will Rogers, I never met a pipe smoker I liked.

"Got a lot of clients, have you, Slots?" He balanced the bowl and cocked his head to one side.

"Are you working with the IRS now, Ackerman?"

"Just trying to be friendly." Morris shrugged. "Maybe I can save us both some aggravation. I don't like aggravation, and neither do you. It's bad for the stomach."

"I don't know what the hell you're talking about."

"I'm talking about Ned Pinto. The word is going around that you're doing some kind of investigation into his death."

Benny! Damn! That guy would do anything for a few bucks. Here I was, burning Ned's pictures to protect him, and he drops a dime to someone at police headquarters.

"Your information is wrong. Tell your friend Benny he made a mistake," I told Ackerman.

"I doubt that. This Pinto was a very big movie star. You always were good at getting your friends on the newspapers to give you favorable publicity. The way I see it, this is a good chance to get even with the department. You're fishing in troubled waters here, Slots. We've got Noolan, and it's airtight. He confessed to everything. He's got the motive, the means, and the opportunity. It's *iron* tight!"

"So how could I cause you any aggravation, Morris?"

"Let's stop fencing, Slots. I know what you're up to."

I figured out what Ackerman was worried about. Pinto and his Russian defector wife, Tanya, had been in town to do their Rally for America at the Garden and the Meadowlands. It was to be a gathering of all "patriotic Americans," designed to show repugnance for communism and the deprivation of freedom. When Pinto was killed, there was an outpouring of public sentiment that it was a Communist conspiracy to silence him. The public, the State Department, Pinto's fans demanded that his killer be brought to justice. When the police arrested Noolan there were the usual conspiracy theorists who refused to accept that the Iron Man's killer was himself a decorated Vietnam veteran.

Vargas, Ackerman, and everybody else connected with the department were busy patting themselves on the back over the successful capture of Pinto's assassin. They weren't going to take kindly to Slots Resnick poking around and igniting the embers of public doubt.

"You'd be doing a disservice to everybody, Slots, if you gave people the impression that there's more to this case than there actually is. Noolan did it, and that's it."

"So now you're the judge and jury, too, Morris. When do you get to be hangman?"

Ackerman didn't answer. He took a long pull on his pipe and blew out little darts of smoke. "I know who your client is," he said.

"Really?" I doubted that. All this fuss wasn't over my teenybopper twins.

"I can save you a lot of time. We've already checked out her story, and there's no corroboration whatsoever."

"Morris, I'm not working for anyone. I'm not involved in the Pinto case."

"You're not leveling with me, Slots."

"I'm leveling with you all the way. Someone wanted to be sure that Pinto was dead. To prove it, I got a couple of pictures of him in the morgue. That was the whole deal."

"Sure. What happened to those pictures?" he asked cagily.

"I burned them."

"Yeah, right."

"It's the truth, Morris."

"You know, Slots, people come into the precinct from all over the city. They've got trouble with their spouses; maybe they think they need protection; they want to have someone followed: there are all kinds of jobs that the department can't do but a private detective can make a fortune on. Now, all I have to do is hand out your card to the desk sergeants in maybe a dozen precincts in the better neighborhoods and there's no telling how many people would be beating down the doors to see you. On the other hand, Carol Simmons probably will stiff you for your fee, and you'll have everybody in and out of uniform pissed at you. Then there's all kinds of problems in renewing licenses. . . ."

"Thanks for the advice, Morris."

"Think it over, buddy boy. You could be making one hell of a mistake if you think you're going to make us look bad."

He got up and went to the door.

"I'll remember that."

I would also remember the name Carol Simmons.

Sherry lived on the twenty-fifth floor of a high-rise in Cadman Plaza in Brooklyn. From her living room window she could look out and see three of New York's East River bridges and the police headquarters building at the Police Plaza. With a good telescope, I might be able to look right into Vargas's office. I wondered if Ackerman would go back and report on our conversation to him.

Sherry looked great in a man-tailored silk suit. She wore Ann Klein originals, she told me, and I said I was impressed. Actually, I felt the clothes she wore tended to make her look much older than her thirty-three years, but maybe she chose that image because of her job. This suit was black and white with a cute little bow tie that she wore over a ruffled white blouse. Sherry had dark eyes—Gypsy eyes, I called them—and black shoulder-length hair.

I had picked her up from work, gone for a bite at The Big Board Café, and now we were back at her apartment. For the past half hour, I was only able to get one-word answers out of her—this was since I'd told her about my talk with Ackerman.

"You do this purposely, don't you? You do this just to annoy me."

"Do what?"

"After Ackerman warned you, why do you have to get in touch with this Simmons woman?"

"Look, Sherry—"

"No, *you* look, Mr. Resnick." I was always Mr. Resnick when we were arguing. "What do I do for a living?"

"You're a financial adviser."

"That's correct. Do you know what a financial adviser does? He or she tries to help clients make money, and *keep* the money they make. I have millionaires for clients. I have people who wouldn't think of investing a penny of their assets until they spoke to me first. Do you know why? Because I'm good at what I do!"

"I don't see why—"

"The only person who never cares what I suggest he does with his finances is you."

"That's not true."

"Oh, no? I told you to invest in IBM at one twenty and what did you do?"

"I bought something else."

"Condutron. Do you know what Condutron is selling for now? I know you don't, because it isn't listed on any exchange anymore. But I don't mind that, Mickey; if that's how you want to spend your money, fine. You know what really bothers me? That you picked Condutron by closing your eyes and taking the first stock that your finger came to. That's really a slap at me, isn't it?"

"No, that's just my method."

"Now, this thing with Ackerman. You *know* that he made you a fantastic offer; you *know* that if desk sergeants recommend you, you can make a fortune in this business. Do you have any idea what a break that is?" Sherry liked to answer her own questions. This time she was waiting for a reply.

"I think that—"

"It's the best damn break you could get! I just can't figure you out. And your reason? Because he gave you a ticket!"

"That was spite, Sherry. He didn't have to have his driver write a ticket."

"So what?"

"That's not the only thing. There was a good reason he didn't want me to see Simmons. There's something that they're worried about. If they thought their case was so airtight, it wouldn't matter what I did. Ackerman came to me for a reason. He overreacted, and I want to find out why."

"Maybe it's a setup. Did you ever think of that? Maybe he knew that you'd get involved and this way they can pull the rug out from under you."

"You're giving them too much credit," I said, but I wasn't sure.

I had been dating Sherry for over a year. We had

lived together for four months at her place and then split by mutual agreement. Her complaint was one I had heard from women for years: I didn't want to make commitments, I only cared about the present and not the future. I had to plead guilty on both counts. That's the way I am, take me or leave me. Sherry couldn't live with that choice, so she separated herself from me.

"At least give it some thought before you do something stupid," she said.

I said I would. I had to admit, though, that the ticket tucked under the Porsche's windshield wiper really ticked me off.

I pulled her over to my side of the couch.

4

• •

By this time, I was as much a Ned Pinto expert as everyone else in the country. You couldn't watch TV without being exposed to a Ned Pinto film festival. People who were part of his inner circle became instant celebrities and were in demand on talk shows all over the dial. The Pinto and Tanya story was headlined in all the tabloids, as well as the weekly newsmagazines, which featured the Pinto Phenomenom. There were two books on the way, and predictably, two major studios were negotiating to film the story of the star's life.

At the time of his death, Ned was thirty-two years old and the hottest star on the Hollywood scene. His last two movies grossed over a hundred million in the States and were still going strong in Europe. *Blood Vengeance* was number three on the all-time box office list, and he collected residuals from the Pinto Iron Man doll, Pinto T-shirts, and of course, the poster of him and Tanya stepping into their Silver Cloud Rolls.

It had been a quick six years since he'd been just

another muscle-bound kid looking for a break. He had landed a bit part in a fantasy-adventure epic having to do with a magical egg and a superhero named Logar. He was one of Logar's men, Odma, who grunted and pointed and was killed when the magical egg fell into the wrong hands. It wasn't the stuff Oscar nominations were made of; it was, however, a hell of a lot better than *Children of the Road*, in which he played a motorcycle freak named Hondo who just grunted, or *Love Deal*, in which he appeared for eleven seconds as a college jock. In that one he never even got a chance to grunt.

It was during *Logar the Invincible* that he met Tanya. The movie was filmed on location in West Germany. Tanya was a lovely, fair-haired girl, on whom most of the crew were trying to put the make. Right from the beginning, though, she made it clear that she was interested in Ned.

A native of Moscow, she defected to the West on a cultural exchange. Russia got to see *Hello Dolly*, and the West had a chance to hear the Leningrad Choir. Tanya seized the moment when her KGB guard was answering the call of nature to scoot from her Bonn hotel to the West German embassy, where she asked for asylum. She spoke German fluently and was granted a visa. She tried her hand at acting and became an extra in *Logar*. Then she fell in love with the heavily muscled American, and the rest was, as they say in the supermarket tabloids, a show business legend.

The fiery Russian immediately took charge of Ned's floundering career. She was persistent and hungry, and after finding a hundred doors locked tight, she found one that was opened a crack. She kicked it down. She accomplished this by hounding a well-known agent until, out of self-defense, he went to see Ned in *Logar*. He wasn't overly impressed, but the muscular young man did have a "kind of quality." He sent Ned to meet a producer-friend-lover who was doing a martial arts thing as a tax shelter and was pleasantly surprised when the producer decided to give Ned the second lead.

The picture might have lain buried forever in the B picture graveyard except for a quirk of fate: as a last-minute change in casting, somebody hired a punk rock group to do the sound track, and one of the songs actually made it to the top of the charts. The music brought people into the theaters, and the critics followed. Some of them singled Ned Pinto out as doing a fine job. Armed with good reviews, Pinto actually had people bringing him scripts to read for his next vehicle.

It was Tanya who chose *Blood Vengeance*. She correctly assessed the mood of the country. People were looking for a new John Wayne—strong, but with a sense of fairness and decency that Stallone's ice-cold Rambo didn't have. It was precisely the right move. Aside from the rave notices, the receipts went through the roof. In movieland, that was the all-important bottom line.

Tanya's touch was infallible when it came to choosing the right scripts. Ned on the screen was to personify the American hero. He was kind and caring, slow to anger, but ruthless and implacable when the things he loved were threatened. Many of the pictures Ned made reflected Tanya's own hatred of communism. There were no gray issues in a Ned Pinto film. The audience always knew who wore the black hats, and they loved it.

The Rally for America was to be a giant reaffirmation of American ideals. From all the reports, Tanya was the force behind the gathering, which was to feature movie stars and politicians, and a plethora of veterans and labor organizations. Pinto was in the paper or on TV every day plugging the rally, which was scheduled to take place in two weeks.

Tommy Noolan had to be the most hated man in the country. He was slightly built, short, with close-cropped blond hair and a dangling gold earring. After seeing the Iron Man wipe out battalions in the movies, it was hard for the public to believe that he could be killed by a punk like Noolan. Evidently the cops had enough to make it stick. The papers had Noolan guilty before the trial. But there was someone who still thought he was innocent: Carol Simmons.

I checked into every paper I could find to get a line on Carol Simmons, but I just drew blanks. I finally got a break when I contacted Tommy Noolan's attorney, Alex Tucker. He was a guy I'd known peripherally over the years. He was competent, but without much flash or imagination. It was obvious that he felt his client was guilty and didn't have much chance of escaping a long prison term. There was no capitol punishment in New York State, so Tucker felt Noolan might get lucky and only have to serve thirty years.

It turned out that Carol Simmons was Noolan's sister. Tucker didn't want to talk too much about her. "You'll see for yourself," he said less than enthusiastically.

The address he gave me was on West Fifth Street in the Bensonhurst section of Brooklyn. The houses were mostly two-family; aluminum siding over wood frames, well kept, with small patches of green yards surrounded by cast-iron gates. I got out of the car and was immediately assailed by a symphony of barking dogs fenced in their own little yards.

Carol Simmons was scooping up the residue of two of her Dobermans. Her house was much more shabby than the others on the block. The area that had once been a yard had been concreted over and served as the lair for the dogs. It was a no-man's-land from the gate to the door.

"I'm looking for Carol Simmons," I told her.

"Yeah? What for?"

She deposited the poop into a garbage can. She was close to thirty but looked older, five feet even, on the chunky side, wearing a shorts and halter top outfit. She had a tattoo of a butterfly on her right shoulder. Her face was pleasant enough without makeup, and there were beads of sweat over her upper lip and brow. She wore her hair tied up in a bright yellow bandanna. Somehow it looked incongruous with her oversize peach-tinted eyeglasses. She hadn't looked up.

"I think I can help her," I said.

The two Dobermans stormed the gate, barking and snarling. The gate was about four and a half feet high, and I wondered if they could jump it.

"Cleo! Portia! Shuddup!" she yelled.

The dogs stopped in mid bark. They looked up at her sheepishly and then set themselves down on the concrete, panting, with their tongues out.

"Who are you?" she wanted to know.

"My name is Resnick. I'm a private detective."

"Thanks, but no thanks," she said. "I don't have money to hire a private detective."

"Let's talk. Give me a few minutes of your time."

"I'm busy." She looked past me at the houses across the street. "Don't that beat all! Look at those bastards spying on me behind their curtains. They got nothing else to do but put their noses in my business. Those bastards went and called the board of health on my goddamn dogs," she fumed. "Sometimes I don't get around to picking up the shit right away. So what? I treat the dogs good, and it's on my property."

"They're great-looking animals," I said.

"Yeah, tell that to the fuckin' board of health. They had the Environmental Control Board give me two summonses." She gestured with her index finger at the houses across the street. "What the fuck you lookin' at? I got my boyfriend here, okay?"

I turned around but didn't see anybody.

"Come on inside with me. I'll give them something to talk about, bunch of goddamn busybodies!"

I walked past the dogs gingerly. They looked up at me but made no attempt to rise.

"They're well trained," I told her.

"Yeah, sometimes."

She opened the door and let me in. The house was furnished in beer cans, ashtrays, and cigarettes. They were all over the place, covering tables, chairs, and the top of a small TV.

"I haven't had time to clean up the place. Have a seat, I'll be right back."

I sat down on a small mauve sofa, which at one time must have been an expensive piece. The wooden arms were scarred by burns from carelessly laid cigarettes. Carol returned carrying a beer. She drank from the can. She didn't offer.

"Now, what do you want?" She sat across from me on a bridge chair, hands on her knees, her chin set aggressively.

"I'm looking into Ned Pinto's murder. I was told I shouldn't talk to you about it, so that made me curious. Maybe you know something that would make people uncomfortable."

"What do you get out of this? Who are you working for?" Her eyes, already glassy, narrowed even more.

"I'm on my own."

"Bullshit! Nobody does something for nothing in this world," she said bitterly.

"If Tommy didn't kill Pinto, there'd be a lot of people who'd look very bad. Let's say I wouldn't mind seeing that."

She made a face. "At least you didn't tell me that you wanted to see justice be served. Give me a fuckin' break! Nobody cares about the truth; they just write a script and match the action to it."

"Tommy's your brother?"

"Yeah, my brother. I hadn't seen him for six years before he came in last week from the Coast. He's a grade-A asshole, but he didn't kill that jerk Pinto."

"You sure about that?"

"Yeah, I'm sure. I told the cops that he was with me when Pinto got shot. He was out in the back getting some sun when I heard the goddamn bulletin on the radio. He didn't leave here until after he heard it on the radio."

"Maybe he stepped out for—"

"Look, Resnick! I'm stoned a lot, okay? I know I'm no rocket scientist, okay? But I also know that my dumb prick of a brother was here the whole morning! He didn't go nowhere, so he couldn't possibly have killed Pinto."

"Did anybody see him here?"

"Probably. Everybody in this stinkin' neighborhood keeps fuckin' tabs on me—but nobody is going to admit it. You got to understand that these people don't want to get involved. I made the cops go around and ask people. Nobody saw nothin'! All day long they're looking out of their windows, taking notes on my whole life, but nobody seen my brother laying in the back the whole morning. How does that grab you?"

"Your brother says he did it. He gave the police a full confession—"

"He's a liar!"

"Why would he say he did it if it wasn't true?"

"How the hell would I know? Why don't you get the fuck outta here, too," she bristled.

"Take it easy."

"Don't bust my chops. I'm telling you, Tommy was here with me. If you don't believe it, fuck you!"

I changed the subject. "Okay, Tommy was a Vietnam vet. That's what the papers said."

"Yeah." She thought about it. "That's what really messed up his head. He served with the Riverines. Did you ever hear of them?"

I nodded. I had heard of the "brown-water navy." They were a tough, ragtag outfit that had seen action in the Mekong Delta.

"My brother was a hero. He got a medal. Did you know that? He hid up to his neck in mud for thirty-six hours and then led his platoon back to their base. You know what Pinto did during Nam? He was four-F because of a punctured eardrum. Give me a break! Tommy hated the fact that Pinto was taking all the credit for being a 'real American' while guys like Tommy couldn't get a job, or collect VA benefits. Sure, Tommy was a junky, but so what? I'd be a fuckin' junky, too, if I went through the shit he did. As it is, I'm a goddamn pothead, pillhead, alcoholic, whatever. My fuckin' husband ran off on me, they took my kid away, the goddamn board of health gives me summonses for not picking up after my dogs. . . . Leave me the fuck alone!" She covered her eyes with her hand.

Carol Simmons was not the kind of witness you'd want to testify if you were building a defense. I wasn't surprised that Tucker wasn't excited by the prospect of her giving Noolan an alibi. A prosecutor would squash her. Yet Ackerman was concerned about something. There had to be something that didn't fit in the police department's investigation, something that could affect the outcome of their neat little scenario. I would have asked her to go on the box had I been investigating the case.

"Did the police ask you to take a polygraph?"

"No."

"They didn't hook you up to a machine? You would have had to sign an okay."

"Oh, yeah. You mean the lie detector? Yeah, I took it."

"What did it show?"

"I don't know. They didn't tell me nothing."

That was it! The box must have said she was telling the truth. Polygraphs weren't allowed to be used as evidence in New York, but the police used them as an interrogation tool. Just the very procedure of hooking up someone to the machine induced confessions. I found the box to be pretty damn accurate. That wasn't to say that it couldn't be beaten. Pathological liars and people on drugs could consistently fool the machine.

Carol Simmons might be one of those people. On the other hand, it would be enough to make Ackerman and the boys downtown wonder if their case was in jeopardy. I knew the three polygraphers the department used. Carol described Jack Butler, who had an office on Atlantic Avenue.

I told her to get in touch with me if she thought of anything else. She nodded and downed the can of beer. I let myself out, walking quickly past the Dobermans, who eyed me suspiciously.

5

· ·

■ got back to the office and played the messages on the answering machine. There were two hang-ups, and a message from Sherry with the ominous *We have to talk.*

She was going to remind me of my financial position and warn me not to make an enemy of Ackerman. Her argument would have a lot going for it. The fact of the matter was that the clients weren't exactly lined up around the block waiting for my services. It seemed to bother Sherry a lot more than it did me, but that didn't mean I wouldn't have liked to be a financial success.

Jack Butler came to the phone after his secretary screened the call. Maybe I needed a full-time secretary. Maybe the clients didn't return after they came to the door and found a business card saying BE BACK SOON.

I traded small talk with Butler, and then I asked him about Carol Simmons. After making me swear he wouldn't be quoted, he told me that her polygraph was "inconclusive."

It was what I had expected. "Inconclusive" was the department's way of saying the results didn't come out the way they expected them to. I thanked Jack profusely and promised him again that I wouldn't compromise him. Everybody was scared shitless of Ackerman.

Then I made a call to Stash. His last name was totally unpronounceable, so to everyone in the detective bureau he was simply Stash. I had gotten him assigned as a detective and it was a decision I never regretted. He was a good cop, and more important, a good friend.

He told me that Boddiker had been assigned to the Pinto case and as far as the department was concerned, it was a wrap.

"What do you think, Stash?"

"This one's clean as a whistle. Tommy Noolan is a wiseass punk, and even if he didn't do Pinto, he should rot in jail anyway," Stash said bitterly.

That wasn't like Stash; he was usually more mellow. Then I remembered that Noolan had also shot J. J. Mitchell. He and Stash had been partners. "How's J. J. doing?" I asked him.

"He's going to be all right. I just come back from the hospital a couple of hours ago. If it wasn't that Noolan's gun jammed, J. J. would have bought it. Noolan got him point blank, right in the gut. It'll be a little while before he's eatin' soul food again."

"Stash, can you get me a copy of the file?"

"Yeah, I think so. But what the hell for? You're not going to try and *clear* that son of a bitch?"

"There're some things that need to be checked."

There was a long pause on the other end. "What's going on, Slots?" His tone was decidedly less friendly. "Noolan's not worth your time."

"I'll judge that for myself. I need the file, Stash. Will you do it for me?"

He thought about it. He didn't like what he was

hearing, but he also owed me. "Yeah, I'll get it to your office myself in about an hour."

"Thanks."

He hung up without saying good-bye.

I had known Stash for twenty years, and this was the first time we had had words about anything. What the hell was I getting myself into? I didn't have a client, Ackerman was going to pull my license, Sherry was pissed at me, Stash thought I was a turncoat. For what? I honestly didn't know. Sure, I would have liked to prove Noolan was innocent and shove that information right up Ackerman's and Vargas's kazoos, but there was something more: something about this case had bothered me even before I'd gotten involved. Call it a hunch. . . .

For a long time now I'd felt like I had forgotten my keys. It's a feeling everybody's had: you walk out of your house and get halfway down the block and you realize that something is wrong, something is missing. It's your subconscious mind screaming at your brain that you forgot your keys. I was having the same kind of edgy feeling about the Pinto case. Or, being such a stubborn bastard, maybe I was just rationalizing.

I put in a long-distance call to California and used some old contacts to put me in touch with the Malibu Police Department. The responding officer on the first attempt on Pinto's life happened to be in at the time, and the captain put him on the line. He had me hold while he checked his notes and then gave me a rundown.

It had happened ten days ago, three days before Pinto and Tanya had arrived in New York. Ned was an exercise fanatic and had taken a dip in his outdoor pool after doing a routine of push-ups, sit-ups, and weight lifting. He was in the process of swimming laps when his wife, Tanya, went out to join him. He got out of the pool and sat down next to her on a poolside chaise.

Tanya saw a man standing on a high sand dune beyond the fence of their property, looking at them. She thought it was a reporter from the gossip sheets. They'd had trouble before from characters with telephoto lenses invading their privacy. She and Ned joked about it.

Ned closed his eyes and the next thing he remembered was that he was thrown off the chair onto the floor. Tanya, who had been watching the guy, saw him raise a rifle, and pushed Ned off the chair just as the bullet was fired. The bullet went through the chair Pinto had been sitting on and richocheted into the concrete. There was no question that had Tanya not pushed him out of the way, he would have been hit. The man with the rifle took off after the shot.

The officer investigated the grounds and found that two barbed wire fences had been cut, enabling the perpetrator to have access to the grounds. Two days later, acting on a tip, they investigated an apartment in Fullerton rented to Thomas Noolan. They found a rifle with a telescopic lens. Ballistics verified that the rifle had fired the bullet that had been intended for Pinto. An arrest warrant had been issued. The New York City Police Department had been alerted, due to the fact that Mr. Pinto was going to be in New York and there was some speculation that Noolan had left California.

That was all the information Malibu had, until they were notified of Noolan's arrest by Detective Boddiker. Details of the attempt on his life had been kept from the papers.

"Then how come we heard about it?" I asked him. "I remember reading how the Iron Man had foiled an attempt on his life."

"I think the studio leaked it," the officer said.

"That's how they do things out here. Anything's okay if it builds up the gate."

"Tell me about the tip you got on Noolan."

"Female voice on the phone. Said we'd find something interesting if we checked out the apartment in Fullerton. That's all we got."

"Okay, thanks."

I gave him my number and told him that if I could return the favor, I'd be happy to.

A few minutes later, Stash rang the doorbell. He handed me a thick folder in a manila envelope. He wore a stern expression. Stash, at fifty-three, was white-haired, with a bit of a paunch.

"I want you to understand—" I started to say.

"Forget it. I'm on my way to see J. J.'s wife and kids. You know he has a daughter now, too. Seven months old. Cute kid. They came this close to being without a father." He held his fingers an inch apart. "You just be sure and do the right thing," he told me.

He walked quickly to his double-parked Fury.

One of the first things you learn is not to trust press accounts. I'd heard the story of Ned Pinto's murder recounted two dozen times on TV and radio; I'd read about it in three different newspapers. Essentially, the versions were all the same. The public hasn't the time or the inclination to hear the whole story. Dramatic headlines sell papers, and "film at eleven" is the shortcut journalistic approach that reduces complicated cases to a couple of paragraphs.

I've sat on cases where innocent people were convicted in the court of public opinion based on lurid testimony from someone with an ax to grind. The media gets hold of that one biased transcript, reduces it to a few sentences, and ignores the volumes of countertestimony that the judge and jury weigh. When the person is acquitted, there is an outcry from all the armchair jurists that someone was paid off, or that so-and-so beat the rap.

I was willing to waive all I had heard about Pinto's death until I'd read the DD5s, seen the reports of the investigating officers and detectives, and gone over all the physical evidence described in the file. Everything was there. The folder was a half inch thick, covering all that had transpired since the Malibu police sent a teletype on Noolan ten days ago.

I could see why Alex Tucker, Noolan's public defender, was so discouraged. On top of all the facts pointing at Noolan, there was his confession, a lengthy diatribe against people pretending to be patriots while the real heroes were denied their place in the American dream. He admitted shooting J. J. Mitchell, admitted shooting at Pinto in Malibu, admitted plotting and carrying out Pinto's murder as the star was caught in midtown traffic.

J. J. Mitchell had made a positive identification that the man who shot him was Thomas Noolan. The bullets dug out of the floor, wall, and Mitchell's belly were from a nine-millimeter Browning. Noolan admitted purchasing the Browning from a friend after arriving in New York. The gun dealer, Chico Rodriguez, identified him. The bullets taken from Pinto's body came from the same Browning.

There were two people riding in the back seat with Pinto when they stopped for a light on Forty-second and Lexington. One was Detective Boddiker, who was assigned to protect Pinto during his stay in New York; the other was Burt Sloan of Command Pictures, the outfit Pinto had single-handedly resurrected. Both men positively identified Noolan as the man on the bicycle who had stuck a gun in the limo window and fired the fatal shot.

I had read enough. As far as I was concerned, I'd find another tree to bark up. Stash was right. Ackerman's nervousness notwithstanding, the case against Noolan was "clean as a whistle."

I tried to call J. J. at the hospital to see how he was doing, but they weren't allowing him to take any calls yet. I called Denise Mitchell and asked her about her husband. She thanked me and told me she'd pass on the good wishes to J. J. Did I know that Stash was there? I asked her to let me speak to him.

"Did you see what you wanted to see?" he asked me coldly.

"Yeah. He's guilty, all right."

"Okay, I told you so." The warmth came back into his voice. "Sorry if I—"

"No apologies necessary. I just want you to know that I'm backing off. Thanks for getting me the stuff."

"Oh, hell, Slots, any time. If there's ever anything I can do, just say the word. You know that."

"Thanks."

The doorbell rang as I hung up the phone. I opened the door expecting to see Sherry. It wasn't Sherry, it was Carol Simmons.

She looked different. Her hair was combed out and she wore a yellow blouse over white clam diggers. The oversize glasses were gone, and so was the glazed look I had seen earlier this afternoon.

"Can I come in?" she asked.

"Yeah, sure."

I led her past the waiting room and into the office, seating her across from me.

"I looked you up in the phone book," she said, looking around. "Nice place."

"Thanks. I'm a little surprised to see you."

She smiled and shrugged. "I get a little stupid sometimes. I've been so fucked over, if someone tries to be nice, it makes me uncomfortable. I wanted you to help me clear my brother."

"Well, Carol, I—"

"I know what you're thinking. You don't think I can raise the money. I will, Mr. Resnick. I swear on my son Gregory that I'll pay you. I'm going to see my mother first thing tomorrow. I haven't spoken to her in ten years. She lives out in Short Hills, with the snob types. She don't care if me and Tommy die. She don't want to know us or hear from us, but I'm going to make her hear me this time."

"Carol—"

"She disowned us. She married some guy that doesn't even know she's got kids. She probably told the guy she was ten years younger than she is and me and Tommy would just be an embarrassment. Well, too fucking bad, right? Tommy's in prison facing a murder rap for something he didn't do. She's got to listen to that, right? You mind if I smoke?"

"No, go right ahead. You told me that you and your brother weren't very close."

"Yeah, we weren't close in the sense that we saw each other often or anything like that. Tommy got in trouble in school when he was a kid, so he joined the navy. He spent a lot of time in the Pacific and settled on the West Coast. I had Gregory, so I wasn't about to go traveling out to California every five minutes, but we kept in touch by phone. I don't write too good, but Tommy wrote beautiful letters. We used to wait for Tommy's letters. I mean, little Gregory used to make me read the letters to him all the time." She paused and took a big drag on the cigarette. "Look, I'm not much on bullshitting. You're a private eye and I'm hiring you, okay?"

"I can't take the case," I told her.

"Why the fuck not? This afternoon you came on like it was some big deal."

"I didn't have this." I held up the file. "It's the police reports on Pinto. I think your brother's guilty."

She looked at me steadily. "You're wrong, Mr.

Resnick. I swear to God he was with me when Pinto was killed. I don't care what your report says. I'm telling you the truth."

"I know you believe that. The lie detector shows that in your mind you're telling the truth."

"So if I'm telling the truth—"

"The DA is going to say that you're a drug addict. He's going to prove that you had a few beers, you smoked a joint, you lost track of time. They've got this"—I lifted the file—"against your unsubstantiated word. And they've got Tommy's confession."

"Just a second." Carol reached into her shoulder bag and took out her wallet. She pulled something out of the billfold. It was a glassine envelope filled with white powder. "You take this. You take this as your retainer."

"Carol, I can't—"

"Just wait a fuckin' minute, will you! That's two hundred bucks of high-grade coke. You take that now, and I swear I'll get whatever you want from my mother. Please, Mr. Resnick. Please. . . ."

I stood up and handed the coke back to her. "Carol, what happened since this afternoon? Why did this become so important all of a sudden?"

"I was stoned."

She gave that as her answer, as if that explained everything. I waited and watched her. She lowered her eyes; when she started talking, I had to strain to hear her.

"It hasn't been easy. I got thrown out of my house when I was sixteen and my mother found out I had an abortion. She didn't care that I'd been fuckin' around, mind you; what ticked her off was the abortion. Strict Catholics, and all that shit. They put me in this home for girls, and I ran away. I didn't have nowhere to go, so I hid in our garage. Tommy would bring me food, blankets when it got cold. I did a little time on the streets, learned how to take care of myself.

"Then I met this guy, Brandon. He was a black dude, a pimp. He wasn't my old man, but I knew he had a string of girls. He always came on to me and I figured he wanted me to work for him, but that wasn't it. He really liked me. Well, a lot of shit went down, and I married him. He got out of pimping and things were working out. I had a kid, light-skinned, but you could see he had some black blood. That was the last time I spoke to my mother. She disowned me.

"We moved into a neighborhood and there was trouble. My kid went to school and the other kids beat the shit out of him. I heard remarks all the time. Brandon was no goddamn help. He was shooting junk now, and totally out of it. I didn't have a person in the world. No friends, no family, and finally, no husband. Brandon left, and my mother worked something out with the department of welfare and they put my kid in a foster home.

"Anyway, through all of this bullshit, I still had Tommy. He wrote to me every week. He called me. He didn't have money to come out to see me, but he said as soon as he could get a score, he was going to fix things up for me. Yeah, I know he was probably bullshitting me, but it kept me going." She looked up at me, and there were tears in her eyes. She fought them back.

"Anyway, like I said, it ain't been easy. When you came to see me this afternoon, I was pissed. I mean, everybody else in my fuckin' life disappeared, including my father when I was five. All of a sudden I was sitting in front of the mirror and I'm looking at myself and I realize I don't have another person in the whole world who cares about me. If I died tomorrow, there's not a fuckin' person who'd come to my funeral."

I handed her the tissue box and she dabbed at her eyes. She balled the tissue up and tossed it into the basket.

"Okay, enough of *This Is Your Life*. I want you to

believe me. I don't care what those papers say. I was with him, Mr. Resnick. He was sitting in the back, taking the sun. I was in the kitchen listening to the radio when they broke in around twelve thirty with the announcement that someone took a shot at Pinto. They didn't say he was killed then, just that he was shot. I went out in the back and told Tommy. He bolted from the chair and that's the last I seen of him until I saw him in court. He told me to keep my mouth shut. I didn't know what he was talking about; then I found out he confessed to Pinto's murder."

"Did he take anything with him?"

"You mean a gun? No, nothing."

"How about clothes he could hide the gun under. He had a denim vest, according to the reports."

"I didn't see that!"

"Carol . . . the evidence—"

"Look, Mr. Resnick. I never asked anybody for anything in my life. I got a funny feeling about you. I got a feeling that you're a straight shooter. I'm not asking you, *I'm begging you*." She held out the coke. "Please . . ."

There are few things in life that are immutable truths. One of the universal laws states that when a confirmed coke user is ready to give up her stash, you have to take it seriously. I told Carol that I would look into the case for her. I wouldn't promise anything, but I'd follow up a little further. I also advised her that she better get rid of the coke because a drug bust would make her that much more of an unreliable witness.

"I give you my word that until Tommy gets off, I'll stay straight," she said.

Unless I could find something to get Noolan off the hook, Carol was going to be straight for at least thirty years.

I got my break-up call from Sherry. It happened just as I took the pillows off the couch in the waiting room and was preparing to hit the sack.

"I called because I couldn't face you in person," she told me. "You'd make me laugh and we'd wind up in bed, and I'd just put it off for another week, or month, or year."

"What's the matter, hon?"

"Our relationship. This isn't what I want for me, or for us. I can't go on waiting and hoping. I love you, Mickey, but I have to love myself a little, too. You can be happy just floating along from one day to the next. I—"

"Sherry, that's all life is, one day to the next."

"Please don't interrupt; I'm finding this hard enough, even though I practiced all afternoon." She laughed nervously, then sighed. "I know you love me, too . . . but maybe I'm just not enough for you. I've thought about us a lot, Mickey. I'm not blaming just you. I'm too independent, bossy. Maybe you need the clinging-vine type, the damsel in distress. You were born a couple of centuries too late, I think. You would have been a great knight in King Arthur's time. Then all you would have to do is save the girl, slay the dragon, and be off on your next adventure." She broke down. I could hear her sniffling.

"What do you want me to say, Sherry?" I asked gently.

"Nothing. There's nothing you can say. I have to know that there's a promise for a future and that's the one thing you can't give me.

"Sherry—"

"Please don't say anything. You've made your choice. Now let me make mine. Sweetheart, please, if you care about me at all, don't call me or try to see me."

She hung up, leaving me with the phone in my hand and the prospect of a long night.

• • • • • • • • • • • • • • • • • • •

6

D etective John Boddiker didn't want to talk to me.

"Don't stick your nose into police business," he said gruffly over the phone.

I couldn't blame him. I had used that same line myself dozens of times over the course of my career, usually to lawyers and reporters who could foul up sensitive investigations. I figured Boddiker had good reason not to want to talk about the Pinto case. After all, he had been in charge of safeguarding the star. J. J. Mitchell was shot and almost killed working under his direct command, and Pinto was murdered. All in all, it hadn't been a good week for Detective Boddiker.

I made my next call to Tanya Pinto at the Grand Hyatt. A man with a deep, oily-smooth voice answered, the kind of voice you pick up on small FM stations late at night.

I fudged over *private*, but I made sure to say *detective* loud and clear.

"Tanya and I have already been interviewed a number of times," the man said.

"May I have your name, sir?"

"Bert Sloan."

"Yes, Mr. Sloan, I know that. This won't take long. I just have a couple of loose ends that I want to tie together. In fact, Mr. Sloan, if you could be there too, it would save me another trip."

"Well, heck. Sure. We'll do whatever we can to help," Sloan said affably.

I took a cab and spent forty minutes in morning crosstown traffic. Ironically, we stopped at the same intersection where Pinto was killed. I pictured it in my mind. It was really more like a political assassination than a murder. Killing someone and escaping on a bike was popular in Europe and Asia; it wasn't your typical New York City homicide.

I took the elevator up to the Pinto suite. Bert Sloan let me in.

"Have a seat, Mr. Resnick. Tanya will be here in a moment."

Sloan didn't fit in with the room's decor. The Hyatt had decorated the suite with geometric patterns in a modern motif. I blazed a trail through the carpet and sat down on a black sofa that was accented by a matching mica coffee table with a brass border. There was a pine scent in the suite, compliments of the maid and Dow Chemical. The art on the walls could fill a small museum, the kind of stuff you see at the Whitney and blink twice at the prices. The far wall was mirrored with a skyline looking like the Magic Kingdom from the old Disney program on TV.

Sloan sat opposite me in a velvet recliner. He was dressed in splashy Vegas. He was about my height, six two, solid, with graying temples and a receding hairline that he tried unsuccessfully to camouflage by combing his hair forward. He wore an open shirt, red and blue, with a huge gold coin dangling from a thick chain. His pants were skintight over white shoes and no socks. A gold watch and bracelets, one with BERT engraved on it, jangled when he shook my hand. He was very tan, with blue eyes over a large nose, and a smile which must have paid for some dentist's European vacation.

He sized me up without giving anything away. "What's this all about, Detective Resnick?" he said, leaning forward.

"Some odds and ends. Nothing very earth-shattering. I was hoping to see Mrs. Pinto, too."

"Tanya will be by in a jiff. She's freshening up. You know, I thought you said on the phone that you were a NYPD detective. You didn't mention that you were a private investigator."

"Oh, didn't I? I thought I did."

He flashed his million-dollar smile, and I threw one back at him.

"Hey, that's no problem. Matter of fact, I'm kind of glad I got to meet you. After you called, I spoke to Mr. Ackerman of the mayor's office. He's been running interference for us here in the city, and he suggested that we *not* talk to you. Then I realized you were *the* Mickey Resnick, and I said to Tanya, 'Shoot, let's talk to the man!' What do you like to drink, Mr. Resnick? Anything I don't have here, I'll call down and have them send up."

He got up and went to a black lacquer bookcase, which turned out to be a well-equipped bar. I told him it was a little early in the morning for me, but he should go ahead. He gave himself a Dewar's, which he poured straight up.

"Fact is, I've heard of you. You caught some psycho who was going around killing clergymen, and you nailed the guys on the Morgan Trust. How much was that, fifteen million?"

"Fifty."

He whistled. "That's a lot of money. Did you ever think of stuffing your shirt and jacket with the money and going south?"

"Sure I thought about it. I'm human."

I had had the money on my desk while we waited for the press to come in and take the shots. The money had been in "bricks," each brick held one hundred hundred-dollar bills. A million dollars weighed twenty-five pounds. A million bucks! I could have been on my way to Brazil. It had entered my mind, but not for more than a minute then—and very rarely since.

"This is going to surprise you. Did you have any idea that we were thinking about doing a movie based on your life? Hey, that was about three years ago; we got pretty close to offering you an option."

I didn't believe him but I looked appropriately pleased. "What happened?"

"I guess something else came along. You know how it is in the movies, one minute you're hot and the next you're not." He shrugged.

"You're with the studio?"

"Yeah, Command Studios. I'm the chief cook and bottle washer. I do a little bit of everything for them, including public relations, which I was handling for Ned and Tanya. Hey, everything is in one hell of a mess now." He shook his head and sighed.

Tanya stepped out from one of the suite's three bedrooms. Bert stood up, so I followed suit. She had the typical California girl look: golden skin and blond hair in a severe cut, which she carried off because of her high cheekbones. Her eyes looked like they were hazel, but they would change color depending on the clothes she was wearing. Today she wore a one-piece white terry outfit, accenting a flawless figure on a five-three body. The nose was too perfect; assistance from a plastic man. There wasn't anything about her that would suggest her Russian roots, nor was there any outward trace of grief.

Sloan introduced us and I made a mental note of her firm handshake as I expressed condolences. She thanked me, and joined me on the couch. Sloan, in the recliner, formed the third leg of the triangle.

Tanya crossed her legs and clasped her hands together. "I will ask you a question first, Mr. Resnick. Who is employing you?" It was a pleasant voice with the assurance that money and power brought. There was a definite accent, but you had to look for it.

"Carol Simmons." There was no need to keep her name confidential. Sloan and Tanya exchanged glances. It was obvious they had never heard of her. "She's Tommy Noolan's sister," I explained.

"Surely she doesn't think that her brother is innocent, does she?" Tanya said, her eyes opening wide.

"That's exactly what she believes."

"And you believe her?" Sloan asked, shaking his head and looking at me as if I had pissed on the rug.

"There's enough doubt to warrant my coming over here and talking to you."

"Hey, bud! I was there, remember? I was there when he pulled the trigger," Sloan snapped.

"I know. Mrs. Pinto, did you positively identify Tommy Noolan as the man who shot at you in Malibu?"

"Yes. I didn't know him then—I mean, know who he was—but it was the same man who tried to kill Ned in Malibu, and the same man who came to the door of the suite."

"This suite?"

"Yes."

"Where was Detective Mitchell?"

"Two doors down," Bert answered. "How's he doing, by the way?"

"He'll be okay."

Mitchell's shooting occurred a day before Pinto

was fatally shot. Boddiker had stationed J. J. in a suite down the hall, with a closed-circuit camera focused down the hallway. Anyone getting off the elevator or coming from the staircase would have been picked up on J. J.'s closed-circuit T.V. camera. The police account stated that Noolan waited in the lobby and then followed one of the room service waiters into the elevator. He decked the kid with a sap to the back of his head and tucked him into a utility closet on the fifth floor. He took the kid's tray and uniform and proceeded up to Pinto's suite, trying to gain access by claiming that someone had ordered food sent up.

Tanya had opened the door just as J. J. came out of his room. He had told room service not to send anyone up on the floor without letting him know first. When J. J. approached Noolan, the report said, Tommy pulled out a gun and took a shot at him. Tanya had enough sense to slam the door as Noolan whirled back. J. J. hit the deck and got a shot off, but missed. Noolan didn't. J. J. dropped his gun and Noolan tried to fire another round at point blank range. Fortunately the gun jammed.

"You were in the limousine with Ned Pinto, weren't you, Mr. Sloan?"

"Yeah. Ned, John Boddiker, and me."

"Is that the order in which you were seated in the back?"

"Right—no. Ned was near the window, I was next to him in the middle, and Boddiker was at the other window."

Tanya's mood was turning to impatience. "Is this leading to something?" she asked.

"How did Noolan know you folks were going to be leaving the hotel right then? Had you ordered the limo to pick you up in front of the Hyatt?"

"He didn't have to know, he could just have been watching the front. Or maybe he was watching the limousine; we'd been using the same one since we arrived. The driver is someone we've done business with for years," Bert said evenly.

I thought about the stretch Lincoln sitting like a beached whale in a sea of traffic, and Noolan gliding by on his bike.

"Noolan sure caught a few breaks, didn't he?" I looked first at Tanya, then at Sloan.

"What do you mean?" Tanya cocked her head to one side.

"The day before he tries to kill a cop, and the next day he hangs around the same place risking identification. Then he follows the limo, lucks into a traffic jam, and rides down the outside lane where Ned was sitting. By the way, the glass on the limo was tinted, so no one could see in, right?"

"Yes."

"So how did Noolan know where to shoot?"

Sloan thought about it. "As a matter of fact, I think that window was open."

"Your idea?" I asked offhandedly.

Tanya fielded the question for Bert. "My husband's, I'm sure. He liked to breathe natural air and preferred not to use air conditioners."

"New York air in the middle of gridlock is a long way from natural air. Noolan—if it was Noolan—sure had a lot of luck."

"It *was* Noolan, Mr. Resnick!" Sloan insisted.

"You're sure you couldn't be mistaken? After all, it happened so fast—"

"No way! He pulled up right alongside the car. I looked past Ned and saw someone on a bike. His right hand was in a sling. All of a sudden, the sling came off and he pointed the gun right into the car. I remember his face; I remember the gun. It was this Tommy Noolan! Boddiker saw it that way, too. Nothing you say is going to change that."

"Bert, I don't want to talk about this anymore," Tanya said, looking away from us.

Sloan reached over and patted her arm. "Of course, dear. Of course."

"I'll be in my room." She walked past me without giving me a glance.

"Hey, I guess that about ends it," Sloan said, shrugging. "Look, I can understand that a sister wants to help her brother, but you can't dodge the facts here. Tanya, Boddiker, Mitchell, me—we're not all crazy. If I thought the real killer was out there someplace, do you think I'd be sitting here? I'd nail that son of a bitch myself! I loved Ned. I loved what he stood for. He was the only guy in Hollywood to talk about what's right about America. This rally would have been the greatest thing going. People would have had a chance to speak out against monolithic lockstep communism. Sure, I heard all the Joe McCarthy jokes they'd been using on Ned, but we were willing to take on the left-wing press because what we're doing is right. You just have to talk with Tanya for a few minutes to really get a picture of the Soviet slave masters and they're puppet governments. That's why Ned was killed! You scratch this Noolan guy a little and you'll find a dyed-in-the-wool Red. I guarantee it! He used the same gun he tried to kill Detective Mitchell with; we all identified him, and he confessed. What the hell more is there?" Bert editorialized as he walked me to the door.

The only thing there was, was the word of an alcoholic, prostitute-doper. So why did I believe her?

7

· ·

I t was eleven thirty when I stepped out of the Hyatt. I blinked at the strong sunlight filling Forty-second Street and made my way to the three public phones on the corner. To the east, past the drive, charcoal gray clouds piled up on top of one another over the Atlantic, and a gust of cold air telegraphed a thunderstorm.

I found one of the phones that accepted my quarter and dialed Alex Tucker's number. The girl said he wasn't in and then backpedaled when Tucker gave her a sign that he'd take the call. "Oh, he just stepped in," she fibbed.

Alex didn't bother saying hello. "So you saw Carol Simmons. You want to put her on the stand, be my guest. In two minutes the DA would cut her to ribbons, and the judge would call me in for a competency lecture.

"She might be telling the truth."

"Prove it!"

"I spoke to Butler—"

"The polygraph man? Come on, Slots, that's inadmissible. You got anything else?"

"No," I admitted. "Just a feeling, and a couple of nagging loose ends."

"Great! I'll use that! 'Ladies and gentlemen of the jury, I want you to find my client not guilty in spite of the evidence that the district attorney has presented and my client's own confession. Slots Resnick has this feeling—'"

"Okay, Alex. You've made your point. I want to see Noolan. Can you arrange it?"

"I'm going over to the Tombs this afternoon to consult with him. It's a goddamn waste of time. He doesn't want to defend himself; all he's interested in is the publicity, so he can get his message to the American public."

"Which is?"

"Which is that the Vietnam vet got a raw deal."

"He just figured that out?"

"Yeah. Thinks he's telling the world something nobody knows. I'm encouraging it. I want him to rant and rave. It gives me a shot at a psycho decision. You want to meet me for lunch? I'd invite you up to the office, but it's just big enough for a game of solitaire if you hold the cards close to your chest. You know Sparky's on Broadway?"

"Yeah."

"Meet you there in an hour."

I felt his shadow before I hung up the phone. He wasn't as big as the World Trade Center, but he didn't miss by much. I tried to walk past him to let him make his call but he came toward me and let me have a short jab with the hard metal he was holding in his hand, despite the draped sports jacket covering it. I didn't have to be Sherlock Holmes to know it was the business end of a gun.

"There's a car parked on the corner. You walk over there like a good guy and take a seat in the back."

I studied his face. If he had the slightest bit of tension in him, it didn't show. His voice was calm, his eyes dull and bored. It was as if he stuck a gun in a stranger's ribs every afternoon. Maybe he did.

I walked to the late-model Seville. It was navy, with tinted windows that were impossible to see through. There were no front license plates. I climbed into the back seat with Godzilla behind me. The driver waited for us to get in and then started down Park Avenue. I could only see the back of his head, oily black hair sticking out of a tan collar.

The big guy was taking his time. He let the gun out for air and pointed it at the roll I had for breakfast. His nose and mouth drooped down to a weak chin, giving him the look of a not too intelligent horse.

"You sure you've got the right guy?" I asked him. "It's a big city, and I've been told that I look like a lot of people. Just yesterday, a woman comes over and asks for my autograph. She swore I was Tom Selleck. Maybe it's the mustache, because I don't think I look like him at all. Another time, somebody figured I was that guy Van something or other. You know, the one who made all the spaghetti Westerns. Even James Coburn, without the white hair. I'm telling you, it's very easy to—"

"Shaddup, Resnick!" the guy driving said. He didn't turn around, but I caught his baby blues in the rearview mirror. His hand on the steering wheel had well-manicured nails, no rings.

"See, I told you! My name is Dave Segal, I'm a professional tennis player. Hey, look, no hard feelings! I hope you find this Resnick guy, because I'm sure he deserves whatever trouble he's in. Don't worry fellas, I'm not going to say anything. Just let me out on the corner and we'll forget the whole thing."

I didn't see Horseface's punch until the very last instant. It enabled me to turn my head just enough to avoid having to sip my food through a straw for two months. It still hurt plenty, and I fought not to go down for the count. It didn't help when one of his big paws went around my neck and he started to squeeze. I put both my hands on his and tried to pull him off me, but it was about as effective as a fly making love to an elephant. I started to see the pretty colors behind my eyes: yellow and black, with splashes of red.

"It's time for you to take a vacation, Resnick. It's time for you to look after your health. A guy like you who doesn't take care of himself could have bad things happen. We don't want that. Nobody wants that. Just leave everything alone and mind your own business; then everybody stays happy. Take this as a friendly reminder."

The car door opened and I was tossed out into the center of the street. I gasped for air and tried to shake the cobwebs out of my head. The Seville sped off in front of me. I wasn't shocked to see that they had removed the rear plates, too. A bass horn caught my attention and I rolled toward the sidewalk, just missing the right front wheel of an oil truck.

I spent the next fifteen minutes pounding dust from my clothes and pulling myself back into shape. My jaw ached. It'd feel worse tomorrow, but at least it lined up okay.

I called in a report about a navy Seville, brown upholstery, tinted glass, in the midtown area with no plates, and left my office number with a desk sergeant I had bent an elbow with on a couple of occasions. Then I hailed a cab. I didn't have much hope that the car would be stopped. These two were pros, and they probably had a garage or a car wash in the neighborhood where they had taken off the license plates and could now put them back on in a hurry.

Friendly reminder!

Alex Tucker was standing in front of Sparky's staring at his watch when I pulled up in the cab. He looked at me and made a face. "Don't bother getting out, Slots. You missed lunch."

At fifty, Alex Tucker was probably the oldest person in the public defender's office. His body was turning from heavyset to fat, and his backside took up more than his share of the rear seat. He was wearing a plaid sports jacket the color of dried blood, and tobacco-colored slacks. He wiped off the beads of sweat on his brow with a crumpled white handkerchief, which he then used to pat the rest of his fleshy face and chins.

He directed the driver to the Manhattan House of Detention, known to all as the Tombs, and sat back and looked at me—and then looked again.

"You get hit by a bus?" he wanted to know.

His small eyes narrowed as they surveyed my jaw. He had thinning brown-gray hair that he combed up from the temples to hide an ever increasing bald spot. His complexion was reddish, with little broken capillaries looking like fine ink lines drawn on his cheeks and nose.

"Something like that." I told him what happened.

"You know what I think? I think it was your pals in blue. I think they believe they're doing J. J. a favor by trying to scare off the guy who's looking to clear Noolan."

I had thought of that. I remember Stash's reaction, and he was a friend. How about all the guys out there who didn't know me? When you're a cop and another officer gets shot or killed on the job, you always personalize it. In the old days, prisoners brought in for shooting at an officer were given a rough going-over in the station's back room. Nobody kept statistics, but those prisoners seemed very prone to resisting arrest or trying to escape. At least that's what the cops said to justify the prisoner's hospital time.

Noolan was out of their reach, but a guy like me, an ex-cop, helping him might be pouring salt in someone's wound.

"I sure hope you're wrong, Alex."

"Believe me. I've seen it a dozen times. The damn Fascists!"

The public defender's office usually was populated by young lawyers out of school who wanted to draw a salary and get their feet wet before starting a practice of their own. Some things about Alex Tucker came back to me. He had come from a wealthy family of attorneys, most of whom were Harvard graduates, and most of whom drew six to seven numbers on their yearly W-2s. Alex became the black sheep by spurning offers of a partnership in the family firm and instead signing on for peanuts as a PD because he felt poor people were getting screwed. Most of the family felt that he'd get tired of it and come back to the fold in a little while, but here he still was, almost thirty years later. . . . Alex paid the cabdriver and waved off my attempt to split the fare.

We went through the security checks. I removed my gun and got a receipt for it.

The conference rooms were on the third floor, drab gray rooms big enough for a metal desk and four metal bridge chairs. The doors were thick wood reinforced with steel, with a glass cutout for the guards in the hall to look through.

Two guards brought Noolan in. They recognized Tucker and exchanged pleasantries, then locked the door behind them.

Noolan was a frail-looking guy who looked more

like a choirboy than a murderer. When they use the term *cherub-faced* they have Tommy Noolan in mind. His curly gold locks framed a perfectly oval face with skin that had never known a razor and a mouth and nose that belonged on a beauty queen. I thought that if Noolan did time, the cons would be salivating over him.

Then I remembered that this Norman Rockwell poster boy was also a war hero who had killed plenty of the enemy and had won a medal for leading his company out of a Vietcong death trap in the Mekong swamps. The tattoo on his right forearm, an eagle holding a skull in one claw and a lightning bolt in the other, also gave testimony that one shouldn't be fooled by his angelic looks.

"Tommy, I want you to meet Mr. Resnick. He's a private detective hired by your sister to help you in this case."

Tommy nodded to me. "Nice to meet you, sir." We shook hands. Then the kid turned his attention to Tucker. "Were you able to get to the press?" he asked the PD.

"No, Tommy. I wanted to look into this Agent Orange thing before I spoke to the press."

"Agent Orange? That was a defoliant they used in Vietnam, wasn't it?" I asked, trying to gain Noolan's confidence, and hoping to get him to open up. According to the police reports, Noolan was raving incoherently about it when they arrested him.

"Yes, sir," Noolan said quickly.

"Tommy believes that the government purposely used the stuff to cause sterility and cancer among the soldiers."

"Were you personally affected, Tom?"

"Yes sir, I was. It was because of Agent Orange that I and many of my comrades had to turn to drugs. I wound up with a one-hundred-dollar-a-day habit, and my sexual desires were completely destroyed."

Tucker looked in a pocket notebook. "Tommy, according to government records, Agent Orange wasn't used in any of the places where you were stationed."

I could see Tucker was unhappy about that; he would have liked to cop a plea based on the claim that the chemical had warped Tommy's brain.

"That doesn't surprise me, sir. I don't expect them to tell the truth." He said it matter-of-factly, as if explaining to children.

"Tommy, why did you kill Pinto?"

He thought about it for a long time, and I thought he wasn't going to answer. I was going to try again, but he finally spoke.

"Because of what he symbolized. He came on as being a supertough guy who could do anything. In his movies, he single-handedly wiped out battalions. That was an insult to all the brave fighting men of the armed services. It pointed us out as failures because we weren't supermen, iron men like Ned Pinto. I heard people say that if we had sent in ten Pintos they would have whipped the Cong alone. Bullshit! He wasn't even in the service. He never lost his manhood or risked cancer.

"All you ever see in those pictures is him killing Charlie and whoring with beautiful women. He was making a lot of money off the men who fought and died. I wanted to show the world how vulnerable Ned Pinto really was, what a phony he was. I wanted the kids to see that it wasn't like that in a real war. Then when I heard he was having that Rally for America, I knew I had to kill him. That was the final mockery of us all."

"Your sister says you didn't kill him. She says you were with her the moment he got killed."

I watched to see if he would flinch. He didn't.

"She's mistaken, sir. I think she wants to protect me."

"You must be a pretty good bike rider."

"I'm not bad."

"Don't be so modest, Tommy. I tried to imagine you riding down Forty-second Street, weaving in and out of traffic, one arm in a sling hiding the Browning. I'm sure it wasn't easy."

"That's how people get around in the Orient, Mr. Resnick. We traveled that way all the time in Saigon."

"When did you leave your sister's house?"

"About eleven thirty."

"You went to the Hyatt?"

"Yes sir."

"Where did you get the bike?"

"Excuse me?"

"Where did the bike come from?"

"Oh, when I got out of the subway, I saw this bike chained to a parking meter. I fooled around with the lock and got it to open. I'm pretty good with a bobby pin or paper clip when it comes to opening locks."

"Your sister says you didn't have a denim vest or anything that you could hide a gun in when you arrived at her house." After the shooting, they had found a denim vest and the automatic rolled up in a garbage can in the IRT station.

"She's mistaken."

"Where'd you get the sling?"

"A drugstore. I forgot the name of it."

"Really? The police say it was a surgical sling. I doubt any Times Square stores would carry that item."

The sling had been in the pocket of the vest.

"Well, one of them did, sir."

I wasn't getting anywhere with Noolan. I sensed nothing in his voice that would lead me to think he was lying, yet more and more knots were coming loose—including the incident in the Seville.

"Mr. Resnick, please thank my sister for me. I do appreciate what she's trying to do, but I am guilty. I really am. If she wants to do me some good, then let her tell the real story of why Ned Pinto had to die."

"Tommy, you're not making it easy for me," Tucker said.

"I know that, and I truly am sorry. I don't want you to have to try and defend what I did. I'm proud of what I did, and I would do it again, if I had the chance."

Tucker looked at me with a what're-you-gonna-do shrug.

We talked in circles for another fifteen minutes and then got up to leave. That signaled the guard to open the door.

I looked directly at Noolan and said, "Whatever the truth is, pal, I'm going to find it."

Noolan smiled that calm, even smile. "You already have the truth, Mr. Resnick. You're really wasting your time."

It seemed there were a whole lot of people concerned with how I spent my time.

Outside the building, the streets were shining from a quick storm, which had blown over minutes after it started. Eddies of quick-moving water rinsed candy wrappers, cigarette butts, peanut shells down into the sewers, leaving the streets momentarily clean.

"How come you know so damn much about this case?" Tucker wanted to know.

I weighed whether to trust him. Eventually, he would have access to everything, but the DAs always stalled as long as possible. I could speed up the process.

"I've got the police reports," I told him.

I saw him chew on that, the wheels turning. "Shit! I guess you wouldn't—"

He wanted a peek, and I owed him one.

"You can come over to my office and take a look, but I can't let you copy anything."

"No problem. Thanks."

We grabbed a cab and headed uptown. Tucker didn't live too far from my place. We got out in front of my brownstone.

"Man! Look at that Porsche!" Tucker said walking over to the spot where I had it parked.

"You like it?"

"What's not to like! I almost bought one, but . . ." He let the words hang as he shook his head. Had he gone in with the family firm, he could have had ten of them. I wondered if he ever regretted the decision.

"It's mine," I told him. "Actually, it belongs to the finance company." I smiled.

"You're kidding! Geez, it's gorgeous!"

At that moment, a spot on the other side of the street opened up. I fished for my keys.

"I'm going to get that spot over there. That's the right side for tomorrow. They have alternate-side parking on this block."

Tucker was running his hand over the hood as if caressing a woman.

"Man! I'd love to drive this sucker!"

"Do you drive a stick?"

"Sure."

"Okay, let her loose, and grab that spot across the street."

"You mean it?" He was like a sixteen-year-old kid. "Can I?"

"Sure. Just hurry up before someone else grabs it."

He didn't need any more prodding. He was in the driver's seat and turning the ignition. I started walking toward my office.

I was lifted and hurled twenty feet by the force of the exploding car. When I picked myself up and turned around, it was already too late to do anything to save Alex Tucker. Nothing could survive that all-consuming inferno.

· ·

I woke up dull-eyed and unhappy, with the whisper of rain on my office window. I was thinking about the night before and a homicide lieutenant named McCoy who had listened to my story four times and had finally asked me to give him a list of people who would have liked to see my card punched.

"What makes you think I could fill a list?" I had asked him.

He was a lean, soft-spoken guy, a few years past fifty, with steady eyes and an icy manner. "A guy like you makes enemies every time he gets up in the morning. Let's go over your story again."

He had been briefed by Ackerman, of course. The guys in the Seville warning me off the case were inconsequential. The bomb in the Porsche was a result of something else; it was just coincidental to the Pinto case.

I broke the bad news to my insurance agent and rented a Nova from an outfit around the corner that took my American Express number over the phone.

When they didn't call back I figured that maybe I had made a payment in the past two months after all.

My brain was just shifting out of neutral when the phone rang.

Nancy was Sherry's assistant, a young dark-haired girl, who had flashed enough smile and personality to let me know that if things didn't work out between me and her boss, we could talk about it over cocktails and pillows. She was a Columbia graduate who was marking off her internship days until she could open her own financial planning office. Sherry liked to put her in her place by asking her to make her phone calls.

"Hi, Slots," she said cheerily. "Sherry wants to talk to you but right now she's wrestling with a bin under the printer that won't stay where it's supposed to. We'll be up to our knees in printouts if she doesn't get it right. . . . Okay, here she comes. Talk to you later, Slots."

I heard some mumbled conversation and then Sherry got on. "Hi."

"Hi yourself. I'm pleasantly surprised. I thought I was taboo."

"Yeah . . . well, I saw an article about you in the paper this morning."

"Oh, no."

"Actually, you made the centerfold. There was a picture of what was left of the Porsche, and about a paragraph on Tucker and you. The story line was that the police were still investigating but were baffled by the attack. I'm sorry about Tucker. Was he a friend of yours?"

I sighed and rubbed my palm over a day's worth of stubble. "Not close, but a friend."

There was a long pause.

"I'm scared for you, Slots," she said softly. "I couldn't stand it if something happened to you."

"I'll be okay."

"What if they try again? Can't you just get out of New York for a while, until the police find whoever it was?"

"No. My best shot is to find out who really killed Pinto. I was warned to keep my nose out of it and when I didn't listen, they tried to get me."

"At least get out of your office. You're a target there. You can stay with me."

She was putting the break-up on hold. I knew Sherry: her feelings hadn't changed, but she wouldn't let me down when I needed her. It was tempting, but I couldn't go along with it. She started to argue but I cut her off.

"Damn it, Slots! I feel so helpless," she said.

"I'll give you something to do. Punch a few buttons on your computer and give me everything you can on Pinto's studio—Command Studios. See what you can dig up on a snake-oil salesman named Bert Sloan. Find out how he's connected with Command."

"Okay," she said, writing down the information. "How long before you can give me something?"

"A couple of hours at the most."

"Good. How about lunch at Dino's?"

"That's expensive; we'll go Dutch."

"Don't worry about it. I don't have to make my Porsche payment."

I called John Clancy at the police lab and asked him about the bomb that had killed Tucker. I sensed something in his voice the moment he knew it was me.

"Okay, Ann, a dozen eggs and a quart of milk," he said.

I gave him my office number and told him to ring me back the moment he could talk. It took about a minute.

"You're a master of timing, Slots. MeCoy was here, and he was just warning me to keep you out of the case when you called," Clancy told me.

"He's following Ackerman's instructions."

"It don't matter anyway, Slots. I got nothing for you. We couldn't really piece much of the device together. My guess is a military plastic explosive set off by a mercury switch."

"Vietnam vintage?"

"Could be, but it's just a guess. It's a real small package and it caused a real big splash. It's not dynamite or anything conventional, like a doctored grenade. No, I'd say plastic, and set by a pro who knew what he was doing."

"Thanks, John."

The phone rang again the moment I hung up. This time it was Carol Simmons.

"I got proof!" she told me triumphantly. "I got a witness who saw Tommy at my place when Pinto was being killed."

"Who's the witness?"

"A neighbor of mine, Dr. Mildos."

It sounded too good. "He's willing to testify that he saw Tommy at your house?"

"That's right! You want to meet him? He's here right now."

"Keep him there," I told her. "I'll be right over."

I picked up the Nova and signed the million papers guaranteeing that if anything happened to the vehicle I'd give my first born as restitution. The attendant, who wore a uniform with HILTON sewn on the pocket, squinted at my address. "Hey, that's where the Porsche blew up yesterday," he said.

I nodded and took the keys out of his hand before he could change his mind.

The car was hot and stuffy with the windows closed. I threw the air conditioning switch and caught a face full of dust. Cursing, I opened the window and continued driving with the pleasure of the dripping rain soaking my left arm.

It took longer than usual to get over the bridge and into Brooklyn, as it always does when the streets are wet. Finally the Manhattan skyline, hidden by low-hanging clouds and fog, was behind me.

It was a little after eleven when I knocked on Carol's door, and that started the dogs barking. She opened the door without asking who it was and led me into the kitchen. The dogs looked up, sniffed, and went back to sleep on the couch.

"I forgot all about Don Mildos. He'd come over that morning, and he saw Tommy taking some sun in the back. Don, this here is Mr. Resnick. He's the private eye that's working with me and Tommy."

The kitchen was neater than the front room, but it was still grimy. There was the smell of dog food coming from a crusted yellow bowl. An insistent tapping sound turned out to be water dripping into a frying pan positioned under a brown-stained ceiling leak.

Don Mildos sat at the kitchen table holding a cigarette in his right hand and a coffee mug in his left. The kitchen set had three matching chairs and a wooden bridge chair. Mildos had chosen the wooden one. He stood up as we were being introduced and carefully placed his cigarette in a ceramic ashtray in order to shake my hand. There were at least a half dozen butts of the same brand in the ashtray; Mildos had been sitting around with Carol for a while.

I shook hands with him and noted the sweaty palm and the limp wrist. In fact, he reeked from sweat. There were beads of perspiration evident on his forehead and his cheeks. The guy looked like he was in a sauna, but if anything the kitchen was cool. He had a moon face with the kind of pale complexion the Chinese call *lo fon*, or "old rice." An unkempt mop of black hair curled around his face in ringlets.

He wore a white-on-white dress shirt buttoned at the collar, even though he wore no tie, and a pair of black polyester pants. I took him to be in his mid forties, although the soft flab around his middle and chest might have made him look a few years older than he actually was.

"Call me Slots," I told him.

"Slots it is," he replied.

His voice was deep, but affected, with feminine intonations. As if to accent the point of his gender confusion, he picked up his cigarette coquettishly between the tips of his thumb and forefinger, his pinky curled in the direction of the ceiling.

"Carol said you were a doctor."

"B.A. from Columbia, grad work and doctorate in American lit from Harvard."

"Don is a poet," Simmons added. "He's even had his poems published in magazines and books."

"I'm impressed," I said, trying to dig up some enthusiasm.

Mildos made a sweeping gesture with his arm as if he were about to make a speech. "Small magazines and cheap books." He shrugged. "There seems to be a conspiracy to keep my work out of mainstream American literature." He waited for my reply.

"That's a shame," I said.

"It's the politics of poetry. I have a word which describes it: 'poelitics.'" He threw his head back and gave a demonic laugh. "Isn't that delightful?" he wanted to know.

I flashed Carol a look and she bit her lip nervously.

"Don, Slots wants to know about the morning you saw Tommy sunning in the back. Remember? That's the morning when Pinto was killed," she prodded him.

"Yes," Mildos nodded. "Yes, I recall it very well. I stopped over to pay Carol and she came here into the kitchen." He pointed to the table. "While she looked in her bag for the change, I walked over to the window and looked out. Tommy was asleep in one of the lounge chairs."

I got up and looked out the window Mildos was pointing to. It overlooked the back yard. Two chaise longues were folded on the strip of concrete.

"You're willing to testify?" I asked him.

"Of course." Again the laugh. It was loud and staccato. It seemed Mildos could turn it on and off like a light switch.

"You're sure that was the day Pinto got killed?"

"Hey, whose side are you on?" Carol asked with annoyance.

"We better be sure our facts are straight. If there's an opening, the prosecutor is going to jump all over us."

"Yes. . .yes, I'm quite sure. I left Carol and walked across the street to my abode. I heard the news bulletin only ten minutes or so after I left her house."

"Thanks," Carol told him. She looked at me nervously. "Why don't you take off for now, Don? Okay? I'll see ya later. Slots and I have to talk."

"Fine, fine."

He got up and went to the door. He seemed shaky, as if he were a sailor getting his land legs. Carol ushered him out offering profuse thanks, which Mildos waved off with a "Happy to help." I sat down in one of the matching chairs and waited for her to come back into the kitchen.

"What do you think?" she asked.

"What's wrong with him?" I asked her.

She shrugged. "Nothing. He's a little eccentric. All those big brains are eccentric. He used to be a college professor."

"And now?"

"He's between jobs," she said.

"Shit!"

"Hey, whaddaya want?"

"How about leveling with me? That guy's got wacko written all over him. Has he really got a doctorate from Harvard, or did you put him up to that too?"

She raised her hand. "Slots, I swear to God! Every word was the truth. He was here and he saw Tommy. Ya gotta believe me."

"How come you never thought of him before?"

She shrugged. "I don't know. Don is like the furniture; he's always around. I just didn't think of him. He's had a tough time lately, but that don't mean he's not telling the truth."

"Why's he sweating like that?"

"It's the medication the doctor gave him," she said.

I put it together. "Lithium?"

"Yeah, how'd you know?"

"That means he's an outpatient. He has to have his blood level monitored."

"So what?"

Ackerman would love this. Nothing like bringing in a paranoid mental patient on lithium to build your defense around.

"He said he came over to pay you. For what?" I asked her.

It seemed to touch a nerve. She looked away. "I don't remember. Maybe some groceries or something. . . ."

"Drugs?"

"No way!"

I got up to leave. "See you," I said.

"Okay, okay. Sit down. I gave him a little pot. I grow the stuff and sell it."

"Terrific. A tree grows in Brooklyn. You gave him a taste earlier in the morning and now he was paying you for it?"

"Yeah." She was wondering what I was getting at.

"You do a joint with him?"

She nodded. "Yeah."

I ran my hand through my hair and wondered about how different my life might have been if I had just stepped out of the way, making the pivot on that double play grounder. I could see the ceremony at Cooperstown. . . . Slots Resnick rising to be inducted into baseball's Hall of Fame. I let the cheering crowd fade from my daydream.

Okay, Ackerman. So psychotic Dr. Mildos wasn't enough for you. Here's another: Carol Simmons, ex-prostitute, drug addict, and cultivator of back yard marijuana.

"Why'd you dummy up, Slots?" she wanted to know.

"You just told me that you smoked grass the day Pinto was murdered. Do you know what a pros-ecutor would do with your testimony if he knew that? He'd tell the jury that even if you weren't lying because Tommy's your brother, you had no idea of time. Marijuana has been proven to distort people's time perceptions. You say you were with Tommy that morning, but maybe you were with him three hours before Pinto was killed, or two hours after-wards, or maybe even another day entirely. I suggest you keep Mildos under wraps, or Tommy won't have any chance at all."

Carol sat looking down at the floor. Maybe she really thought she had something. Maybe she knew she was just clutching at straws.

I got up feeling a hundred years old and swam the thirty yards through the storm to my car. My hand froze as I stuffed the key into the ignition. I sighed, and stepped out again into the rain. I lifted the hood and made sure the ignition wires were going directly into the starting motor without any detours. Of course, the thing could have been rigged to blow as soon as the hood was lifted, but I'd counted on

Tucker's murderer not having that kind of insight into human nature.

I slid behind the wheel and nosed the car back in the direction of Manhattan. Along the way I made a stop at a drugstore and bought a roll of Scotch tape and pasted a strip in such a way that if the hood was lifted, it would break the tape.

I wondered if the insurance company would give me a deduction in auto rates because of my new alarm system.

9

Dino's was over on Fulton, not too far from the South Street Seaport and within walking distance of most of the Wall Street brokerage firms. It was a little after twelve when I pulled the Nova into the lot and handed the guy twelve bucks for the privilege of parking my car for about an hour.

I said hello to Bianca, who with her husband Phillip owned Dino's. They had borrowed the money to buy the place from a rich uncle in Sicily, and he'd made them use his name as part of the deal. Even in Sicily everybody wants to see his name in lights.

The restaurant had two levels. The noisy walnut bar was on the street and catered to the three-button folk who were looking to network themselves with the movers and shakers of the corporate world. These were the ambitious types glad-handing one moment and then looking furtively around them as they whispered some hot new rumor into the ear of a barstool compatriot.

The downstairs was more relaxed, frequented by

manager types in parties of fours and fives. These had graduated from the frenetic action of the upstairs bar and now were concerned about their golf scores and vacations on the Cape.

Bianca squired me to a table in the back that had more or less been our regular station whenever Sherry and I met for lunch.

"A Budweiser for the gentleman and white wine for the lady when she arrives," Bianca told a gold-coated waiter who was placing menus and filling the water glasses. "How have you been, Mr. Resnick?" she asked.

"If you've got arthritis, no sense kicking," I offered.

She thought that was hilarious and walked away repeating it to herself.

I killed five minutes reading the backs of the sugar packets. Everything I always wanted to know about the great sailing ships of the nineteenth century was lying there in the bowl. As an added bonus, I found out that the rose was the official state flower of New York, and that orchids were only fertilized by hummingbirds.

Sherry walked in, and more than one middle-aged gent paused in mid sentence to watch her walk toward me. She was wearing a yellow dress that looked like a parachute, cinched at the waist with a thick, gold-studded leather belt. She slipped into the booth next to me and the material made a swooshing sound that reminded me of a gust of wind through a field of long grass.

As she sat down the waiter brought over her white wine and my beer. She took a sip from her glass and stared at me. "Well, you look none the worse for wear. I see you've got a bruise on your chin, but outside of that you look to be in one piece."

"How about giving me a more thorough examination," I said, throwing a pass she chose to ignore.

She had a look of quiet exasperation that she had developed during the time we were together.

"I've got to tell you this Slots, even though I know what your answer is going to be. A guy I know was on the phone with me this morning. He's got an idea about opening a nationwide chain of superfast auto service stations. You pull in and four mechanics go over your car, change the oil, lube, whatever. You're out in ten minutes. He calls it the Pit Stop, and he's going to open them all over, like McDonald's. His problem is that he needs a good guy with ability and brains to help him get the thing started. We're talking six figures, Slots—six figures and nobody trying to kill you!"

"Then it's no fun."

Sherry sighed and gave me the I-don't-know-what-I'm-going-to-do-with-you look. She tossed a manila envelope onto the table. "Here's the lowdown on Command Pictures and Bert Sloan," she said, settling back against the cushions. The stack of papers, clippings, and pictures was close to an inch thick.

I was impressed. "Imagine what you could do if I gave you more than a couple of hours."

"Our research department is top-notch. We have major newspapers and most of the major news-magazines cross-indexed in our data base. It's just a matter of pushing the right buttons."

She paused while the waiter took our orders. I thumbed through the material and ordered the tortellini; she had a light salad.

"How about breaking it down for me," I told her.

She took another sip of wine. "Your Mr. Sloan is a very shrewd operator. He started with three partners about ten years ago. They made low-budget horror flicks and science fiction stuff that cost them next to nothing and brought them back a very modest return on their investment. One of the pictures they made was a bomb called *Devil Lover*. It played in a couple of drive-ins, had a limited run on the B picture circuit, and faded from memory."

Something clicked for me. "Hold it! I remember that picture. It wasn't a horror movie, it was a light comedy with some sex queen—they were all known as blonde bombshells then. Got it! Jennifer Baker."

"Wrong picture."

"You mean there were two *Devil Lover* pictures?"

"Sloan's movie had been on the shelf for years when MGM was scheduled to release their Jennifer Baker picture. They had just spent close to four million putting together an advertising package including TV, radio, newspapers—you name it, when their lawyers received a letter stating that Bur-Slo Cinema was going to rerelease *their* film."

"Wow."

"Yeah, wow. MGM had a choice; give Sloan a king's ransom to destroy all copies and the master of his film, or throw out the four million bucks already spent on ad spots, not to mention retitling their picture, and respending four million to publicize the new title."

"How could that happen? I'm sure the big studios must have people who check to see that—"

"This one fell through the cracks. MGM's lawyers tried to prove that the woman in charge of the research department had received a bribe from Sloan. You can't copyright a title, and Sloan's flick was hardly a household name, so he figured why shouldn't he try to muddy the waters and maybe cash in on the deal. He could never win in court about using the title first because of the nontitle copyright laws, but he could confuse the public and make some money on his film. Moviegoers would buy tickets because of the title on the marquee, not realizing it wasn't the MGM film. If MGM allowed that to happen it would sure as hell siphon off the profits on their film, and the public outcry at the deception could totally destroy their credibility with the people who buy the tickets. In the end they signed a production deal with Bert, as well as gave him two hundred thousand for complete rights to his film."

"Was the woman bribed by Sloan so that she wouldn't advise MGM of the title similarity?" I asked her.

"Bur-Slo Cinema produced about twenty movies; each one of them was owned by Bert and his other partners. About six months before MGM's picture was to be released, Sloan bought all the rights for that one picture from his partners. It was the only picture he owned solely. This all came out in the negotiations. Sloan said he had always liked that particular film of his and so he had decided to own it outright. It was perfectly obvious he had inside information, but knowing something and proving it are two very different things."

"What happened to the woman?"

"MGM fired her, of course, and then she disappeared. I understand she's now living in Florida and doesn't seem to have any money worries."

The waiter brought our food. I took a swig of my beer. I had my own method of choosing which beer I should order. The one with the least offensive commercials got my nod. Lately though, I had to admit that those Clydesdales were getting on my nerves.

"Where does Pinto come into this?"

Sherry nodded; this was something she liked to do. She enjoyed learning about a company, knowing its assets, its liabilities, the reasons for its success or failure. She wouldn't like it if I pointed it out to her, but substitute *people* for *corporations* and you could just as well call yourself a detective.

"I told you that Sloan had a deal with MGM as part of the settlement. What it came down to was that Metro agreed to distribute three Command pictures a year. Oh, did I tell you that Bur-Slo had now become Command Studios, because Bert bought out each of his old partners? You see, making a movie is just a small piece of the total deal. The success of a film depends on its distribution. For a small percentage, MGM would use its own distribution network to get Command pictures into the theaters."

"That's a big deal for Sloan, huh?"

"To put it into language you could identify with, it's like jumping from class-D minors to the Mets."

"He still needs money to make pictures. Two hundred and fifty thousand gets burned up in a hurry in that business."

"That's the beauty of the deal he signed with MGM. Once word got around that he had a distribution piece, people wanted to throw money at him. If a Command picture made money, it was going to make it big. If it lost money, well, this was still in the days of the fat tax write-offs. Investors figured they had a good downside position with the potential of maximum return if the picture took off. In other words, they stood to make a lot more money than they could lose."

"How the hell did you learn about all this stuff so fast?"

"That's my business: to be a quick study and sound like I know what I'm talking about." She had that funny look on her face again.

"Yeah, but there's something you're holding back."

She smiled. "Okay, I thought I'd impress you. Two years ago there was a messy divorce case involving Sloan and his wife. She sued him for a bundle and he countersued. The L.A. *Times* gave it full coverage and most of the background I'm giving you came from their story, which ran for about three weeks."

"Infidelity?"

"What else? He with a twenty-year-old super-senior from UCLA and she with her plastic surgeon. She got a big settlement."

"Yeah, middle-aged jurors hate to see a guy with a twenty-year-old. The women feel threatened that it will happen to them, and the men are so jealous they figure he doesn't deserve the money too."

Sherry thought about that and shrugged. "Anyway, one day Tanya Pinto comes in holding a print of some film her husband just made. She gets to show it to Sloan, and although he wasn't blown over by Ned he decides he likes Tanya's concept of the patriotic American hero. It turns out he's fed up with antiheroes and Pinto might just fit the bill."

I remembered Sloan's right-wing speech at the hotel. "He also has the luxury of using other people's money," I chipped in.

"And you say you have no business head," she said patronizingly. Pinto makes *American Warrior* and the Iron Man hype takes hold. He makes three more pictures for Command and with the MGM distribution, they take off like rockets. Command Studios now becomes one of the largest independent film companies in the country."

"So Sloan doesn't work for Command, as he led me to believe; he owns the whole shooting match."

"Not quite. Here's the interesting part. Sloan has two partners, and each gets a third of the profits."

"His ex-wife."

"That's right. Would you like to try for the grand prize?"

"Ned Pinto."

"You really are a detective, aren't you? Tanya wrote up a contract that gave Ned the rights to a percentage instead of a salary. The contract was for a one-shot deal only. When Sloan wanted to do the next picture, Tanya wasn't interested in salary. She wanted Ned to get a piece of the action. Sloan is no fool. He figured a third of millions was a better deal than sixty-six percent of nothing."

I thought about that as I picked at my tortellini. "With Pinto out of the way, Sloan stands to make a lot of money."

"Wrong. Command Studios put out seven pictures last year. The only one that made money was Pinto's. With Pinto dead, Command Studios is kaput. He was their only marketable commodity. Their stock dropped from sixty on the NASDAQ to thirty-five in three days. Besides, Tanya inherits all of Ned's assets, including his third in Command."

"So Tanya wouldn't want Ned offed either," I mused. "With Ned dead, her golden goose was gone, too. Besides, all she had to do was take a swim when she saw the man pointing a gun at her husband back in Malibu. By pushing him off the chair, she saved his life."

"Now what?" Sherry asked me.

"Coffee and a piece of that pecan pie."

"No, I mean where do you go with the case?" She was like people with snakes: they claim they hate the reptiles but can't take their eyes off them.

"I'm going to read all this stuff you gave me and then take it from there."

She checked her watch. Since she had done most of the talking, she hadn't eaten more than two or three mouthfuls of salad.

"You hardly ate," I told her.

"I know. I'll have to grab something later." She stood up and looked down at me. "What do I tell the Pit Stop guy?"

"Wish him a lot of luck."

She made a face and nodded. "That's what I figured."

10

Back in my office, my feet up on the desk, I took a deep breath and exhaled slowly. The papers Sherry had given me were balanced on my lap—except for the one in my right hand, the one with the picture that had the hairs on the back of my neck vibrating like strings on an electric guitar.

I looked again at the shot. It was taken from a *Time* magazine, circa 1984. The article had to do with the Iron Man phenomenon, which was beginning to steamroll back then. The picture showed Pinto in a Roman legionnaire costume, holding a sword in his well-muscled right hand. The tag under the photo said *Pinto mania! Will the Iron Man turn to rust?* It was a still from one of his early movies and it was just one of ten or fifteen in the pile of clippings and reports that Sherry had supplied me with.

What made this one important and had my heart pumping like a lottery winner was the actor directly behind Pinto in the photo. He was a head taller than Ned and wearing a gladiator costume, with what looked like an old aviator helmet on his head. I recognized his face: I had seen it up close in the back of the Seville when he made an impression with his knuckles on my chin.

I scanned the article for the second time to see if I had missed the name of the picture. It wasn't mentioned.

I thumbed through the Rolodex until I came to Jan's name and number. She was one of my teeny-boppers from Shreveport who headed the late Pinto fan club. It took a few moments to explain what I needed to know. She listened to the description of the picture and told me that it was definitely *Hero of the Arena*. I thanked her and assured her that the article in *The Midnight Reporter* that said Ned was alive and living in a Tibetan monastary wasn't true.

I trekked down to the video store on the corner and had the counter girl help me find the movie, which she told me was in great demand since Pinto's murder. "That was before he had his nose job," she said. "He's still cute, though."

I shelled out the five bucks that they charged in Manhattan to rent a movie overnight, and once back in my office, I slipped it into my VCR. I gave the Forward Search a workout until I came to the gorilla I was looking for. He was playing a gladiator named Marcellus. What little doubt I still had evaporated the first time he opened his mouth and spoke. It was the same dull voice that had warned me to stay out of the Pinto case.

I skipped to the final credits and waited for his name to pop up on the screen; I missed it the first time and had to roll them again. Marcellus was played by Bill Wackley.

There was no listing for Bill Wackley or William Wackley in the Manhattan book and I drew blanks in the other boroughs, too. I tried Actors' Equity, who told me to send a letter and they'd check on it. Then I thought of Command Studios.

One of the stories in Sherry's portfolio mentioned a Hal Epstein. I gathered that Epstein was active in L.A. and had a casting agency that supplied much of the talent for Command pictures. I called California, but they never heard of Wackley. I tried the New York office of Command and juiced up my story by telling them that I was casting commercials and old Hal Epstein suggested I give a call to line up Bill Wackley for one of the spots. My hose job got me nowhere, until I mentioned that Bill was one of the folks who'd starred with Ned in *Hero of the Arena*. "That was the picture right before Pinto got his nose job," I said to prove my knowledge of the movie biz.

"Hal Epstein told you to call us?" the female voice on the other end asked, and the pitch went up the scale.

"Yes, ma'am."

"Well . . . I can't imagine. Hold on and I'll look in our files."

I waited without much hope. The wheels in my head were already spinning as I tried to figure out my next move.

"That's William Wackley," she said, sounding as if she were reading the name from something.

I perked up. "Yes. William or Bill."

"Well, I have something here. We do payrolls in this office, you see, and I send out the W-2s. He's worked in quite a few pictures. Funny, I don't recall his name."

"You'd know his face," I said. "Do you have an address?"

"No, sorry. We used to send his checks to his agent, who deducted his fee and paid Mr. Wackley directly, but there haven't been any in quite a while. Is he an elderly man with a very large nose?"

"No, he's a big strapping guy. We're doing a commercial for the, uh, wrestling industry. We want to get more people involved in the sport."

"Well then, it's not the fellow I'm thinking of. He'd be crushed if one of those big bruisers fell on top of him. Is it fake?"

"You mean, are the matches fixed? Well, what do you think?"

"I think it's real. I've been arguing about that with my mother. She's eighty, bless her heart, and she tells me I'm foolish to watch those men pretending to be angry and flopping all over the floor."

"You're right, and the dear old lady is mistaken. What did you say the name of that agent was?"

"Myron T. Kupper, thirteen forty-nine Broadway," she told me.

I thanked her and dialed Information for Kupper's number.

The secretary on the other end sounded bored and wasn't impressed by my commercial deal. Mr. Kupper was in conference for the rest of the afternoon and wasn't taking phone calls. She told me to call back tomorrow, or write a letter.

I flagged down a cab and we bucked the crosstown traffic to Broadway. I had expected an office in a skyscraper and I was right, except you wouldn't get any nosebleeds going up to Kupper's Theatrical Representation on the second floor. The directory in the lobby said 210.

The carpet in the hall was light brown, worn to a tired nap at the entrances to the three offices to the right of the creaky elevator. I didn't see any numbers on the doors.

There was the smell of cigars in the air and a more urgent odor of ammonia as an elderly black man in a blue uniform filled a bucket with water from a slop sink on the other side of the hall and gave me the once over. I asked him which was Kupper's office.

Without breaking his whistled rendition of "Blue Moon," he pointed to the first door with a long bony finger and turned his attention back to the sink.

The door was unlocked and led into a cubbyhole of an outer office. There were two tired lounge chairs, one with a slit in its phony leather showing the white of its foam rubber guts. The other had a sagging middle, giving evidence of long years of servicing the backsides of Kupper's show business clients. The rest of the decor consisted of a nicotine-hued love seat covered with see-through plastic and a modern-looking desk.

The tired secretary looked up from her *People* magazine without missing a beat on her chewing gum. She was young, about twenty, with pleasant features that were spoiled by a practiced look of bored contempt. My guess was that Kupper didn't keep her around because of her business skills. "Can I help you?" she asked.

"I'd like to talk to Mr. Kupper."

" 'Fraid not," she said, clicking her gum. "He's tied up in conference. He won't see ya without an appointment, and I know you don't have an appointment since you're not in the book."

"I think he'll see me," I told her, just buying time while I figured out which one of the two doors in the office led to Kupper's inner sanctum.

We both heard the sound of a woman laughing. It was a delicate tinkle, like good crystal brought together in a toast.

"Conference?"

She shrugged. "He's seeing actresses for a new movie. You an actor or something?"

"Something. I'm a detective and I have to see your boss. Why don't you be a good little girl and call him out for me."

The "little girl" jibe ticked her off. You could see it

in the way her mouth tightened. She thought for a second, then pressed a button on the phone console.

A man's voice came through. "Yeah! " he said in annoyance.

"There's a guy out here who says he's a cop. He wants to talk to you."

"You see his badge?" the man asked her.

She looked up at me. "You have a badge?"

I fished in my wallet and put a card down on her desk. She looked it over. "He's a private detective."

"Tell him to screw off," Kupper said.

She looked at me with satisfaction. "Why don't you be a good little boy and screw off."

"Sure." I went toward the door where I'd heard the woman laughing.

"Hey, stop!" the secretary screamed.

I tried the knob, but it was locked from the inside. It wasn't much of a lock. I kicked it right under the jamb and the door seemed to explode open.

Kupper was sitting in the middle of the room with a script on his lap. The Asian woman sat across from him, reading from another script. She was attractive, with long black hair halfway down the back of her white sweatshirt. He was fat and florid-faced, with salmon-colored hair that grew in a perfect circle around a saucer-sized bald spot.

"What the . . ." he mumbled, staring up at me.

"Sorry to break in on you Mr. Kupper, but I'll only take a minute of your time."

"You get out of here or I'll throw your ass out!" he bellowed.

"I tried to stop him!" the secretary called from behind me.

"I just want some information on Bill Wackley. A minute of your time and I'm history." I watched his reaction at the mention of Wackley's name: he knew him, all right.

Kupper reached into his shirt pocket for a cigar

while he thought it over. He went over to the Asian girl and took her hand. "You give Candy your name and number, Kim. I'll let you know," he said to the actress.

She got up and nervously walked past me.

"I'll call the cops," Candy told him from the door.

"Just close the door and get out of here," he said.

"Oh, sure." She slammed it hard, cursing under her breath.

Kupper got up from his chair slowly and made his way to an oak desk on the far wall. Behind the desk there was a gallery of photographs, all black-and-white, all signed with inscriptions. I recognized Bob Hope, a very young Sinatra, Jack Benny, Alan King, and Lucille Ball. Myron Kupper was in each photo, shaking the star's hand or sharing a laugh.

"What's you name?" he asked me. He finally got the cigar going. I recognized it as the same hunk of rope that had stunk up the hall.

"Resnick."

"Why do you want to know about Bill?"

"He a friend of yours?"

"Oh, yeah. A great friend." He spit a piece of tobacco over his right shoulder.

"You know where I could find him?"

He leaned forward. "You got to give to get," he said, staring me down and blowing out a cloud of white smoke.

The room had been close before the cigar; the Asian girl had worn an inexpensive perfume, and Kupper had on the heavy scent of musk. I went over to the lone window and stared down at the traffic backing up on Broadway when a U-Haul van got caught in the intersection as the light changed.

There was a soft scraping sound coming from the desk where Kupper was sitting. I turned fast and kicked in the drawer, closing it on his wrist before he could bring the gun up all the way. It dropped out of his hand as Myron clutched his wrist with his good hand.

"You son of a bitch! I think it's broke," he wailed.

"Tough." He wasn't badly hurt. Kupper was playing for sympathy.

I bent down and picked up the hammerless Browning .25. I checked it. It wasn't for show. The magazine was loaded.

I slapped him hard across the face and knocked the cigar across the room. "Sometimes I'm too polite," I told him. "People don't understand when you're too polite. They take it as a sign of weakness." I slapped him again, this time knocking him off the chair.

"Hey, take it easy, okay? Just take it easy." He held up his hands in front of his face. He was breathing hard, his eyes wide with fear. "What the hell do you want to know?"

"Tell me about Wackley."

Kupper shrugged his shoulders. "I know Bill. Got him started in the business. He couldn't act his way out of a piece of tissue paper. He came to me a few years ago and he begged me to get him some work. He was a big, dumb kid, a jock, no talent. I felt sorry for him, y'know? I'm a sap for a sob story. It's a failing of mine."

He gingerly touched his cheek, which was beet red. "I hooked him up with Command Studios and he lands a part in one of the early Pinto pictures. Now he doesn't have any use for me anymore. He's making connections, because he and Pinto become bosom buddies. I got a contract with him but he acts like it doesn't exist. I must have missed out on a fortune because of all the extras he pulled in. Pinto said he was his good luck charm. He gave him a spot in every picture he made. He went into business with him. Bill was the guy who got the rights to the doll—you know, the one with Pinto dressed up in the T-shirt and jeans. I got a clause in the contract that says I should get a piece of that stuff, but he stiffed me." Kupper puffed on the cigar and shook his head at the memory.

"You should have sued him," I said.

"Sure! Sue Bill. Sure. That's all I'd need. He likes to hurt people. He gets a kick out of it, like other people get from sex. You think I need him breaking my legs?"

He reached out for the chair and lifted himself up. "I haven't seen him for over a year. The bastard borrowed a grand off me and never paid it back. I finally asked him for it and he told me to get lost."

"Where does he live?"

"I've got an old address. I got to look in the desk drawer."

He reached into the drawer and pulled out a small address book. He wrote down the address and gave it to me.

"What'd Billy do?" he wanted to know.

I didn't answer. Instead, I tossed the Browning back to him after taking out the magazine.

"I'm going to pay Billy-boy a visit. If you warn him that I'm coming, I'll be back here and I'll be very upset."

"Don't worry. He's the last guy I'd do anything for. I hope you kill the bastard," Kupper said, looking sour and rubbing his cheek.

• •

11

Wackley lived in a four-story walk-up between Chinatown and Little Italy. I found the right front door on my second try and climbed the dank stairs to the top floor. There were three apartments and a sealed door that had once been a dumbwaiter. The floor had been mopped at least once since the Depression and the hall was illuminated by a naked sixty-watt bulb suspended from a frayed wire. Wackley might have been Pinto's pal but that sure didn't help him out financially.

I checked the scrawled names on the plates of the doors. Apartment A was Lopez; B was Chin; and that left me with my boy Wild Bill Wackley in C. The process of elimination, my dear Watson.

There was a buzzer or bell connection that I pressed without any audible response. The Lopezes were having a vehement argument in Spanish and the sound of a toilet flushing was Chin's audio contribution to the scene. I knocked loudly, waiting for some kind of reply, but Wackley wasn't answering.

The door was the solid-wood type, reinforced by a steel frame. The lock was an old Segal, nothing fancy, but a tough bird to kick in without disturbing the neighbors. It was too thick a bolt for the celluloid strip I kept in my wallet, and although I carried a set of lock picks, contrary to popular belief it was a royal pain to coax the pins into the right position. There was a fire escape that led down from the roof, but my feeling was that in this area, the roof and top floors would be well protected.

I tried the knob, and to my surprise it turned. I opened the door six inches or so and looked in. The entrance led into a narrow foyer branching out to a room on the left out of my line of vision. I eased my hand into my shoulder holster and pulled out my Detective Special, letting it fall to my right side as I opened the door wider and stepped into the place. I waited, standing perfectly still and listening for any sound. There was the methodical ticking of a dripping shower head and a slightly muffled Mrs. Lopez cursing in the adjoining apartment.

I moved quickly, hugging the wall till I reached the cutout of the room on the left. I could see most of the apartment now. There was a nook of a kitchen, surprisingly clean and organized; an open door that led into the bathroom; and two feet from where I stood, the combination living room—bedroom. I bent low and took the two steps that brought me into the open.

Bill Wackley was there all right, staring at me with three eyes. He was sitting at his table, the sun streaming in on a slant through a rip in the dark shade that covered the window. A shaft of bright yellow spotlit his face.

I holstered my gun and went toward him. His third eye, the one weeping red, was in the center of his forehead, put there by a large-caliber weapon at close range.

He had been in the middle of dinner. There was a plate of spaghetti on the table, some garlic bread, and a pot of coffee. I touched the cup; still warm.

Wackley had been a very neat person. The only thing that looked out of place was the other chair. It had been pushed away from the table and tipped over on its side. The killer had to be someone Wackley knew and trusted. There was a full cup of coffee across the table from him, where the other chair had been. The handle pointed to the left. A lefty?

Wackley had been in mid chew when he was killed. I could see a strand of spaghetti still in his mouth, and his fork was still in his hand. The killer had been invited to sit at Bill's table; Wackley poured coffee for both of them. The killer liked his black. I tasted it, dipping my finger into the tepid liquid so as not to put any prints on the cup. No sugar. I filed away that piece of info. People usually took their coffee the same way all the time.

I went through Wackley's pockets and came up with seventy-five cents in change, a folded telephone bill (no long-distance numbers listed), a broken pencil, and a money clip holding eight bucks. He had to have a wallet somewhere, and I spotted it on a weathered steamer trunk next to the convertible sofa. There were the usual number of credit cards, some in the name of William, some in the name of Bill Wackley.

Nothing else seemed of any interest, except for the card from Command Studios. It was gold-embossed and had ARLENE DIAMOND, PUBLIC RELATIONS printed on it with a New York number. On the back were two other numbers written in different colored inks, hastily scrawled. One was local and the other had a California area code.

I pocketed the card and poked around the apartment, trying to get a feel for the kind of guy Wackley was. A chest of drawers held a dozen carefully folded shirts and four sweaters. There was an underwear drawer and another drawer that held ties and belts. Everything was folded and lined up, like a classy men's shop. A closet held five different pairs of shoes all standing at attention in a perfect line. There were three inexpensive suits, a couple pair of slacks, and two blazers—one blue, the other brown.

Except for the clothes, nothing in the apartment could be described as personal. There were no books or records or any bits of memorabilia from Wackley's past. I opened the steamer trunk and found more clothing, winter stuff. I gave up checking the pockets of the coats after finding nothing in the first two: Wackley wouldn't put anything away without checking the pockets very carefully.

I thought about the gun he had pulled on me. That would have to be in the apartment somewhere. I checked the closets again and the sofa bed. No luck. I looked under the table and in the kitchen. I shook cereal boxes and opened the freezer on his ancient Amana.

That brought me back full circle to the steamer trunk. I looked behind it and saw the gun laying against the wall. It was a Smith & Wesson Combat Magnum, fitted with barrel underlug and chambered for .357 magnum cartridges. One of the bullets had been fired, and from the size of the hole in Wackley's head, it was a pretty good bet that Wild Bill had met his end looking down the barrel of his own gun.

The phone rang, loud and insistent. I carefully slid the gun back behind the steamer trunk and lifted the phone off the hook. I waited for someone to speak first, but they were waiting for me.

"Yeah," I said, trying to sound as if I was yawning, to camouflage my voice.

"Bill? Bill, is that you?" It was a female voice. A nervous voice that was vaguely familiar.

"Mm-hm," I answered. I waited again, but this time I got nothing for my time. I found myself holding a dead line.

There was some scurrying outside the door, and finally a heavy knock. I drew my special and waited.

"This is Lieutenant MeCoy of the police department. Come to the door and throw your gun out," he called.

"Take it easy, MeCoy. It's Slots. The coast is clear; you can join the party," I told him, opening the door.

He walked in gingerly, his service revolver cradled in both hands. Two uniformed officers followed. They looked like kids, barely out of the academy.

He saw the gun in my hand and followed my eyes to Wackley's body. "You ice him?" he asked, giving me the fish-eye.

I shook my head. He reached over and took my gun, sniffed it, and counted the bullets in the chamber. He handed it back to me. "Put that away," he said. "Guns make me nervous."

MeCoy looked over Wackley's corpse while the two young cops stood a respectful distance away and practiced their Bogart expressions.

"I know you've got a lot to tell me, Slots, so how come I don't hear you talking?" MeCoy said.

I told him about spotting Wackley's face in the video and tracing him to this apartment. "He was dead when I got here. The coffee he was drinking was still warm, so I figure it must have happened within the hour."

"You didn't see anyone? You didn't hear anything?"

"Just the couple next door screaming in Spanish. But what brings you here? Dropping in for coffee?"

MeCoy shook his head. "We got an anonymous.

Gave this address and said we'd find a body and the killer. He also said it was tied in with Pinto's murder."

"Well, that seems to be the way to get action," I said ruefully. "They ought to stick it on the phones next to nine one one: 'For better service, mention the Pinto murder.'"

If I thought that would get a rise out of MeCoy, I was wrong. He started walking around opening closets and looking in Wackley's drawers. "You toss the place already?" he asked.

"Yeah."

"I figured. You want to be a good guy and tell us what you found? It'll save us all some time, and these kids have to get home early for their cookies and milk." He nodded in the direction of the two rookies.

"Behind the steamer trunk. It's Wackley's baby cannon. I have fond memories of him jabbing it into my kidneys the other day."

He lifted the steamer and saw it. "Hey Desmond, pick this thing up with a pencil and put it in a plastic wrapper for me."

One of the young cops deftly placed the revolver in a plastic bag.

"One of the bullets is missing, Lieutenant," the kid said.

"No it ain't. It's right there in Mr. Wackley's skull," MeCoy deadpanned. "You got your prints on the gun, Resnick?"

"No. I lifted it by the grip where you couldn't get a print."

"How do you see it?" he asked me.

"It's got to be someone he knew well. He invites him in, offers him some food, some coffee. The killer accepts the coffee and when Bill goes into the kitchen for a cup, the other guy gets up and pulls out the Magnum from behind the trunk."

"Maybe the gun's on the table all the time," MeCoy offered. "Wackley doesn't like to eat with it sticking in his belt, so he puts it on the table, and our killer just picks it up and blows him away with it. After he kills Wackley he wants to hide the gun, and so he tosses it under the trunk."

"No," I said. "That was Wackley's spot for the gun. There's an imprint of the weapon in the carpet which tells me he kept it there."

MeCoy thought that over and then took a look at the imprint himself. "What else you know?" he asked me.

"Just that I'm tired, and I could use a little dinner."

"Hold out a few minutes longer. I got my orders to keep you on ice."

"Why's that?"

"An old friend of yours wants to chat. Why don't you take a seat on that sofa over there and give us a few minutes."

I knew he meant Ackerman, of course. It took about five minutes before the smell of his Sail tobacco preceded him into the room.

Ackerman made a point of not looking at me. He chatted quietly for a few minutes with MeCoy while I cooled my heels and then waited for the lieutenant and his entourage to walk out of the apartment.

Ackerman was wearing a khaki sports jacket with leather patch sleeves over a pair of brown slacks. A new addition was the gold wire-rimmed glasses, which along with the thinning gray hair, made him look older than his fifty-five years.

He walked over and pointed the stem of his pipe at me. "Well, my friend, it looks as if you've bought yourself a peck of trouble this time," he said smugly.

"I don't see it that way." I kept my tone even.

He stared at the corpse for a moment and then pulled up the overturned chair, straddling it from behind, his hands resting on the back. "The way I see it, you've got a murder one to worry about, my brash friend. This fellow threatened you, and you tracked him down and killed him."

"You know that's a crock. And by the way, you shouldn't move the chair before it's dusted and photographed." I got up and started for the door.

"I'm going to have MeCoy haul you off to jail, Slots. You should have listened to what I told you."

I whirled around. "Let me get this straight, Morris. You think you can pin this on me?"

Ackerman shrugged. "You've got a motive, you've got the means, and you've got the opportunity."

"You know damn well I didn't plug our boy here."

"Maybe you did and maybe you didn't. The point is, I can have you tucked safely away for your own good. You'll have a chance to do some reading; maybe you can write your memoirs."

"Your case against Noolan is full of holes, isn't it? You're so damn scared you'll try anything to keep me out of it."

"Don't flatter yourself, Resnick. The Pinto murder is solved. We don't need hotheads like you to get the public riled up. We don't want an international incident to occur in this city."

"What the hell are you talking about?" I asked him.

He took a long draw on his pipe while he decided if he was going to tell me. He opted not to. "We don't have anything else to discuss," he said prissily.

"Have it your way," I said. "I'll read about it in the papers, I'm sure. Why don't you tell MeCoy to come in here and snap the cuffs on me."

The mention of the newspapers had the desired effect on Ackerman. I could see the smug look dissolve into tight lines of apprehension.

I pushed my face close to his. "It's going to be a big story, Morris. Maybe front page, with banner headlines: 'Ex-Chief of Detectives Arrested for Murder.' I'll be out on bail by tomorrow and I'll have one hell of a press conference. The mayor is going to love it. There are a lot of things people might get curious about, like how come Carol Simmons passed a lie detector test when she was asked if her brother was with her? Or where did Tommy get the surgical sling he was wearing? Or the bike?"

I watched Morris's face. It was a calculated shot, but I was right. The cops must have grilled every pharmacy in the city without any luck, trying to link Noolan to the sling. There probably wasn't a report of a stolen bicycle either.

I followed up my advantage. "Then I'll talk about death threats, and how I was set up to look like I killed someone. Somebody will put the pieces together and come up with a police conspiracy as the bottom line."

Ackerman thought it over. "Maybe we're prepared to take the heat," he finally said. "Noolan did kill Pinto. I'll grant you that we don't have every *i* dotted, but that happens sometimes. There are times you never have all the facts, but that doesn't stop you from getting a conviction. Why don't you do yourself a favor Slots, and sit this one out?"

It was becoming a tired refrain by now. I had heard it from Sherry, from Stash, from Wackley, even from poor Alex Tucker. I thought about Tucker. I had sat in the back of the funeral home and paid my respects in my own way. A piece of me was with Tucker in that closed coffin. I was glad his family didn't know who I was. I stayed as long as I could and walked away.

"I'm a funny guy, Morris. When I get pushed, I want to push back. I was the one they were after when Tucker turned the ignition in my car. I'm the guy who you're threatening with a murder rap."

"Oh come on, Slots. I know you didn't take me

seriously. We go back too far for that kind of thing," Morris backtracked without missing a beat. "We're concerned about this Rally for America getting out of hand." He was the earnest, concerned Ackerman now. He spoke quietly, sharing what was on his mind. We were just two old friends, and he wanted to fill me in on what was going on. The man was amazing.

"After Pinto got killed all hell broke loose for the first couple of days," he said. "There were threats on every Communist embassy in the city. We needed a hundred extra men to guard the families of just the Cuban and Libyan missions. We had to surround the compound the Russians have out on the Island. We intercepted letter bombs, and there was a mysterious fire or two that may or may not have been set by right-wing terrorists. Our feeling now is that the Libyans might try to stage something on their own so they can milk it for propaganda. You see what we're worried about, Slots?

"On top of everything else, Tanya Pinto is determined to go through with the rally. We've gotten reports that every right-wing nut from the Klan to the Birchers is going to be in the city. There are busloads of anti-Castro Cubans coming up from Florida. We've got anti-Communists from Afghanistan to Zanzibar all flocking to beat the drums against the Communists. We don't want to see the city turned into an inferno, Slots. All these people need is an excuse, any excuse."

"Tommy Noolan was a godsend, wasn't he?" I thought out loud.

"The climate being what it is, it was fortunate that Ned's murderer was to the right of the political spectrum, rather than to the left," Ackerman agreed.

MeCoy knocked and stepped into the apartment without waiting for a reply. He handed Ackerman a sheet of paper. "Thought you might want to see this," he told the mayor's man.

Ackerman looked at the sheet, nodded, and handed it over to me. "Mr. Wackley had quite an arrest record," Morris said.

I looked over the rap sheet. He had four priors for loan-sharking and burglary. He had done time in his native Wisconsin for second-degree manslaughter. There was a dishonorable discharge from the Marine Corps in the late sixties and on the bottom of the sheet was a cross-referenced file on Wackley kept by the Justice Department. I memorized the number and handed the sheet back to MeCoy.

"Thanks, Lieutenant," Ackerman said patronizingly.

He waited for MeCoy to walk outside. "What I'm saying Slots is that I hope you'll have an understanding of what's at stake."

"You mean, don't rock the boat."

"Slots, you made a good point before about publicity. Quite frankly, I hadn't thought it through. There's something else you can consider: lawyer's fees today run into the tens of thousands of dollars, even for innocent people. Then there's the matter of having your private investigator's license renewed, as well as your pistol permit approved. In addition, we have our own sources in the media."

There was another knock on the door.

"Forensic team is here," MeCoy called in.

"I take it I'm free to go," I said to Ackerman.

He nodded. "For now. I'm not bluffing, Slots."

I pushed my way past MeCoy and made my way down to the street. The first chance I got I jotted down the Justice Department reference number from Wackley's file. There was a phone on the corner. I pulled out the card with Arlene Diamond's name on it and dialed first the business number, then her home number. No answer. I checked my watch: It was after five. She might have been in transit from work.

For no apparent reason I thought of Sherry. I decided to call and thank her for the lead. Maybe she'd be willing to meet me for dinner.

Her line went unanswered, too.

. . . .

climbed into the car and drove around until I could find a parking spot near a restaurant. It turned out to be a greasy spoon on Houston Street. I was served a cup of mud to go with my undercooked burger and I tried not to think about the taste as I mulled over the events of the afternoon. The highlight of the lonely repast occurred when the brassy waitress in the short skirt bent over to clean the adjacent table.

I kept going over the anonymous call to MeCoy. It was someone familiar with the Pinto case, that's what he'd said. That probably excluded Wackley's neighbors. The killer also had seen me go up to the apartment. There had been no one on the stairs, and the apartment windows had been locked from the inside. It had to be someone who knew me.

My thoughts drifted to the other man in the car when Horseface Wackley told me to take a vacation. The driver had matted black hair, blue eyes, and well-manicured hands with no rings. I burned up the memory banks trying to recall if I had seen anyone who looked like that near Bill's house. I drew a blank, but whoever it was had seen me—and knew me—otherwise he never would have known I was there to see Bill.

I remembered that there was a telephone booth near Wackley's apartment I had used to call Diamond and Sherry: that might have been the phone Wackley's killer used to call the cops when I pulled up a few minutes later.

While I was thinking about phone calls, I tried again to place the voice of the woman who had called Bill's apartment. It had been strained with tension. It could have been someone calling to warn Wackley; it could also have been someone at that corner phone booth.

I paid the bill and watched the man standing next to my car. He hadn't seen me come out of the restaurant. He was of medium height and build, with wet-look black hair. Wackley's partner in the Seville?

He peered into the car and then looked around to see if anyone was watching him. I ducked behind a mail drop and wondered about the brown bag he had tucked under his arm. Explosives?

I waited until he worked up the courage to look for the lock under the hood. There were seven car-lengths between us as I walked into the gutter and circled around. I saw him reach into the bag and stick something on the left side near the starter.

I was practically on top of him when he noticed me. I jabbed the special into the small of his back, enjoying his startled grunt of pain.

"Hey, what's going on, man? *Que fue?*"

This guy's eyes were brown—brown and bloodshot. If he was my man in the Seville he was wearing colored contacts and had picked up a pretty convincing Spanish accent. His pores oozed booze.

I stuck my head under the hood at the spot where I'd seen him working and pulled out a set of cable cutters. This guy wasn't looking to blow the car up, just to steal its battery.

"Hey, come on, man! I'm trying to make a buck so's I don' haf to go back on the welfare, man. That's degrading shit!" he told me.

"You're plucking at my heartstrings," I said, patting him down and coming up with two quarters, a penknife, and a gas station business card with *Delco Freedom Battery* written on the blank side. The Lower East Side Sunoco had its own way of supplying parts for their customers' cars.

"What do they give you for a battery?"

"Ten, and a bottle. I'm sorry, man. You gotta keep that gun on my neck, man?"

I holstered the weapon and pushed the wino down the block.

"Hey, give me back my clippers, man!" he said, rubbing the spot on his back where I jabbed him.

"Where do you want them, in your nose or in your ear?"

"Dey cost me money, man!" he said belligerently.

"Call it a business expense; you can deduct it from your taxes."

I pulled away deep in thought, driving on automatic pilot, steering and accelerating, cutting in and out of lanes without any conscious realization.

I found myself driving up the ramp of the Brooklyn Bridge in the direction of Sherry's apartment at Cadman. There was a stationery store on the corner and I stopped in to buy a chocolate heart and one of those "So Glad We're Friends" cards.

I should have picked something up from the doorman's expression when he pulled open the filigreed door. He looked at me, nodded, and seemed to want to say something but thought better of it.

"How are you, Brian?" I asked.

"Fair to middlin'," was his pet expression, and he didn't change the script.

I survived the elevator's music and rang the bell on Sherry's door. She opened it and gave me an uncomfortable smile.

"Hi," I said, extending the chocolates.

She stared down at the gift-wrapped heart, finally taking it. "You should have called, Slots," she said quietly.

Her nervous glance back over her shoulder told me all I wanted to know.

"Company?"

"Yeah, a friend from work. I cooked some dinner."

"No problem," I shrugged. "You're right, I should have called." I turned and walked down the hall.

She caught up to me at the elevator. "Hey, look Slots, you're not going to make me feel guilty!"

"I don't want you to feel guilty," I told her.

"I have to get on with my life, Slots. I can't wait for you forever." There was the slightest note of desperation in her voice.

"Right."

I pushed the button on the elevator. It must have been on the moon.

"You're hurt," she said, reaching out to touch my shoulder.

"I'm fine. Have a nice dinner with your friend."

The elevator doors finally slid open and I stepped inside.

She gave me a hard stare. "Always the ice cube! Everything rolls right off you. What would happen if you showed some emotion?"

I sighed. "I don't know what you want from me, Sherry."

We stood looking at each other during the eternity it took for the doors to close.

"I don't know what I want from you either, Slots . . . except for you to just care. Here! You can take this." She tossed the chocolate heart through the closing doors. "You've been playing around with mine long enough," she said.

John's Bar was within walking distance of my office. It wasn't a dive, exactly, but if you were looking for ambiance, you wouldn't find it at John's. The place was as unpretentious as its name. It was a blue-collar bar, most of the trade uniform-clad men from an elevator repair business and a plumbing outfit.

John Ramirez was a heavy Hispanic with a swarthy face set on a bull neck. His close-cropped salt-and-pepper hair had a lot more salt in it today than in the days I knew him as a fine detective at the precinct. A bullet in the chest took him out of the lineup, and he and his wife, Mary, purchased the bar from Frankie Ryan, when he left loan-sharking for a more lucrative career in real estate.

I found a spot along the long oak bar in front of the honey-roasted almonds and polished off a tall beer. John nodded hello but with that sixth sense all good bartenders have decided to keep his distance. By the third beer I had made a significant dent in the almond bowl and I started to tune in to the conversations around me.

A thin man balancing a cigarette between his lips was moaning about his boss while his buddy in a hard hat nodded and made sympathetic noises. Another guy was putting down the way his wife was bringing up their kids.

"Who did Maris hit his sixtieth off? Anybody know?" A fellow in a rear booth posed the question and groaned as the answer came back: "Jack Fisher."

"I told you! Hand over the twenty," the girl with him said, laughing.

I took it all in, part of it and yet far away. Slots Resnick, resident ice cube, busy analyzing, weighing; an outsider with no room for anyone else in his tight little world. Easy Slots, don't crawl into the beer glass. You know what it is to get caught up in the trivial nonsense that fills the lives of most people.

Remember how you felt when the doctor passed the death sentence on you? You looked back on a life of trying to fit in according to everyone else's ideas. Follow the rules and get by. There's got to be more than that. Okay, so now you make your own rules. Are you happier? Has anything really changed? No complaints about how the wife spoils the brats. Maybe it would be nice to have brats to spoil.

"Another one, John. What did they do, lower the alcohol content in these things?"

Feeling really sorry for yourself, huh, Slots. That doesn't match your MO. You're supposed to be the Teflon detective; nothing sticks to you. No emotions, no pain, no blood and guts. It all rolls right off your back. Slots Resnick, resident ice cube.

You've got to make the pivot faster on that play at second. You cross the bag and whirl. The shortstop feeds you shoulder high, and you're already moving, gliding out of the way of the sliding runner, floating in the air like a ballerina. You fold your legs under you as you make the throw to first.

Who did Resnick hit his sixtieth off?

Crawl out of your beer glass, Slots. No ice cubes in a beer glass.

"How you doin', Chief?"

"Gettin' by, John. Thinking about what might have been."

"There's only what is, my friend."

John filled the almond bowl and walked down the line to the next troubled soul. He didn't look the part of a philosopher, but with a bullet lodged an inch from his aorta, he qualified.

Drink up, Slots. Time to go home.

13

knew who it was the moment I saw the long legs emerging from the cab. She paid the driver with a ten and didn't bother with the change. It must have been quite a tip: the driver said thanks and touched the brim of his hat.

I froze at the door, the key in my hand.

"Mr. Resnick, I was hoping I'd find you here," Tanya Pinto said. "I know it's after office hours, but I thought I'd take a chance. If you weren't in, I thought perhaps you'd have an emergency number where you could be reached at home."

I didn't bother to tell her that the office was my home. Instead I said something about picking up some files and invited her in.

She was wearing a cocoa-colored silk blouse over a yellow shirt and boots. Her severely cut blond hair was in a style that not more than one woman in a thousand could wear well. On anyone else it would have been butch, more fitting for a well-corseted matron with biceps. On Tanya, it was strikingly feminine. She had the face and figure that guys begin dreaming about when they graduate to puberty.

She sat herself across the desk from me and looked around my office. She sat very erect, very businesslike. This was no cream puff; this was the brains behind Ned Pinto. This was the lady that owned a third of Command Studios.

"I pictured something different," she said. "I guess I thought your office would be more . . . well, maybe art deco."

"That's part of the territory. People think of private detectives and they think of Philip Marlowe and Sam Spade. I've been toying with the idea of getting a pebbled-glass door and stenciling 'Resnick, Private Detective' on it. Maybe I'll put in a coatrack so I can pull off my hat and toss it onto a hook while I call my secretary Dollface."

She made a down payment on a smile and looked away nervously. The third button on her blouse was open and I made a conscious effort to pull my eyes away from the revealed cleavage. No bra for Tanya.

"I don't know where to start," she finally said.

I did. I recognized the tense voice. It was the same voice I had heard over the phone asking for Wackley in the dead man's apartment.

"What did you want to talk to Wackley about when you called him this afternoon?"

"What?" Her smoky blue eyes widened in surprise. "How did you know?" I saw her stiffen. "Of course: it was you who answered."

"You know he was murdered."

"Yes, I got a call from McCoy, the homicide lieutenant. He asked me some questions. He mentioned that you were there. . . ." Her voice trailed off. "Mr. Resnick, I want to trust you."

"Call me Slots, and I'm a very trustworthy guy.

You didn't come here to redecorate my office. What's on your mind? Maybe I can help."

She decided. "All right. Here, look at this." She reached into her handbag and came up with a folded piece of paper, which she flattened on my desk and handed over. It was regular three-holed loose-leaf paper with a picture of a hammer and the letters ULWC written in red ink. Under the heading were the words *Enemies sentenced by the people to die!*

The list contained four names: Ned Pinto, Bill Wackley, Tanya Pinto, and Bert Sloan. Ned and Wackley's names had red lines drawn through them and EXECUTED printed next to them.

"When did you get this?"

"It came in the mail this morning."

She fished in the bag again and pulled out the envelope. It was a plain envelope addressed to Tanya at the Hyatt. The pen it was written with was an everyday ballpoint and the postmark was Manhattan, mailed yesterday.

"I thought it was someone's idea of a sick joke at first, but then I felt I should call Bill just to tell him about it. When someone else answered, I thought I had dialed the wrong number. I was going to call him back but I decided I was being silly. Then McCoy called me and told me the horrible news."

I held both the letter and the envelope up to my desk light. The police lab could do a thorough analysis and come up with clothing fibers and dust and the like. Ninety-five percent of the time it was a complete waste of time.

"You have any idea about this hammer and ULWC?"

She shook her head.

"I'm worried, Mr. Resnick. I'm the next one on the list. I don't want you to misunderstand me, however. I am a soldier. We are all soldiers, and I have consciously put myself on the front line against communism. People must be made to understand the nature of the implacable enemy we face. If I am killed, or Bert, they will have achieved their goal of destroying the Rally for America."

"What about Tommy Noolan?" I asked her. "If the ULWC—whoever the hell they are—killed Ned and Wackley, that would mean Tommy was innocent."

"Unless he was one of them. I believe there's a conspiracy, Slots, and Noolan was a double agent. The KGB has done this before."

The beer had dulled my brain, but not so much that I couldn't see that what she was saying might be true. Lee Harvey Oswald had been called a Communist stooge and a right-wing fanatic. For people like that, the ideology was secondary to the fanaticism.

If Noolan was part of some Red organization, then Wackley's warning me off the case wasn't because I was getting close to unearthing something that would clear Noolan, but for some other reason, like a sense of misguided loyalty to his good pal Ned.

Then who wired the Porsche? Wackley might have wanted to do something to make himself feel better about Ned, but I couldn't see him trying to kill me. If he wanted me dead, he could have done it in the Seville and dropped my body off the Canarsie pier.

That brought me back to the ULWC, whoever they were. Why would they want to see me dead? If they didn't want Noolan to be linked with them, why send a letter? If they wanted to kill me, why wasn't my name on Tanya's laundry list?

There was another explanation for the Porsche bombing that I wasn't happy with, but it still had to be considered: maybe McCoy and Ackerman were right and the bombing wasn't at all related to Pinto. I had been a cop a long time and it wasn't always a job that lent itself to being the most popular boy in the class.

"Why me, Mrs. Pinto? Why not talk this out with your buddy Ackerman. You certainly didn't seem too thrilled with me in the hotel room, and I can't believe my boyish charm captivated you into calling on me."

"I can't share this with the police." She put her hands on the arms of the chair and leaned back. "Once the police learn of this organization, it will only be minutes before someone leaks it to the press. The Rally for America would become a media circus."

"It would seem to me that that would be precisely what you'd want," I told her. I couldn't say it, but Ned Pinto's murder and the subsequent publicity was making the rally one of the major events of the decade.

She read my mind. "Ned's death has already given us all the publicity we want. There's a very real danger that the rally could be canceled if the mayor felt it would pose a threat to the tranquillity of the city."

"There's not much chance of that happening," I told her.

"No, you're wrong. They're looking for an excuse, and the possibility that armed men might be in the audience at the Garden's Forum would be all they need. You see, the State Department is putting on a lot of pressure. They still believe they can deal with the Communists and they're afraid that our rally would poison the atmosphere for a new proposed summit meeting."

I could see her point. Headlines about some mystery organization claiming to have killed Ned and Wackley and threatening to kill Tanya and Sloan would sell a lot of papers.

"What makes you so sure I won't leak this to the newspapers?"

"You've already been active in the case, and Bert knows about you. That's the reason I came to see you and not anyone else. Bert says you have a reputation for being a man of integrity. He also said you were very good at what you do. He was once thinking about making a movie about your life."

"What does Bert say about the letter?"

"He laughed it off and said not to pay attention. But that was before Wackley was killed."

I stood up and walked around the desk, where I sat on it facing her. "What exactly do you and Bert want me to do?"

"The Rally for America opens in two days. I would like to be alive for it, and so would Bert. If you could find these ULWC people and bring them to justice, so much the better."

I tossed that around for a moment. Tanya, Ned, and Sloan were all principals of Command Studios. Wackley was just a small-time actor. Where did he fit as an "enemy" of some fanatic group? I thought about Wackley and his friendship with people at Command, particularly Ned. Then I remembered the card in his wallet.

"What can you tell me about Arlene Diamond?" I asked, watching her face closely.

Diamond worked for Command Studios and Wackley had her home number. Questions can be like oil rigs: you can put them all over a tract of land and come up empty. But this one delivered a gusher.

Tanya's eyes narrowed and her lips tightened. For a split second the cool veneer cracked. "That bitch! She's a pathological liar. You can't believe anything that woman says!" With an effort, she regained her composure and looked up at me. "What has she told you, Mr. Resnick?"

"Not very much," I hedged.

"I'll bet!" The eyes blazed again.

"Why don't you fire her?"

"We can't! It's written into the settlement agreement. Do you think I would have her around one second longer than I have to? It's not enough that she gets a third of our profits, but she has to meddle in the business as if she knew what she was doing."

The light bulb in my head clicked on. I remembered

Sherry's report: Arlene Diamond was the former Mrs. Burton Sloan. The PR job gave her something to do while she watched out for her own interests.

"What was her relationship to Wackley? I understand they were pretty close friends." Drop another drill into the ground, Resnick.

"Then you understand more than I do." She clammed up, as if she realized I had been fishing and maybe she had said too much already. Reaching into her pocket, she brought out a roll of hundreds held together by a rubber band and handed it to me.

"You have three thousand dollars there. Will that be enough to insure our safety and your. . .confidentiality?" Her smile could have melted the polar caps. "You don't have to give me an answer now," she said. "Call me in the afternoon and let me know. In fact, why don't you join me for lunch tomorrow, in my suite. Would one be too early?"

"No, one is just fine."

Just then there was the sound of a high-pitched pulsebeat, a sound that was difficult to place.

"That's my daily five thirty vitamin alert," Tanya said, touching a button on her watch, which stopped the alarm. "May I have some water to swallow these with?" She held up a vacuum-sealed packet containing an assortment of pills. I gave her a glass of water and watched her swallow all of them.

She smiled again. "I like you, Mr. Resnick. I find you a very interesting man." She rose, and I walked her to the door.

As she stepped outside, she turned and touched my cheek very softly with one outstretched finger. It was sexy as hell.

"I'll see you tomorrow," she breathed.

The scent of her perfume lingered in the office, heady and sensuous.

14

atthew T. Clarke started his career as an aggressive young prosecutor out of the Manhattan District Attorney's office. It didn't take much of an eye to note that the barrel-chested black lawyer was a good one. When the FBI was looking to reorganize the New York office, I passed on Matt's name with a high recommendation. He worked his way up the ladder to the position he held today of assistant director for New York City and the six northern counties and Long Island.

He was in his office early this morning. When he heard it was me on the phone, he asked for my phone number and called me back ten minutes later. It sounded like he was calling from an outside phone.

"What's wrong with the phone in your office?" I asked him.

"I'll tell you when I see you. You've got to need something, am I right, my man?"

I told him what I wanted and let him know that I

would understand if he didn't want to take a chance. He cut me off and mentioned a diner on the West Side not too far from his lower Broadway office.

I killed ten minutes waiting for him by trying to balance my saltshaker on its edge. The trick was to spill a little salt on the table and then place the shaker down on top of it. Somehow the grains of salt managed to hold the shaker in balance.

"What the hell are you up to, Chief?" Matthew asked, sliding into the booth and knocking over the shaker by jostling the table.

"Nothing at all, Matt. How are you?"

"Paranoid. That's why I couldn't talk to you on the phone. There's talk about the CIA having our office bugged. I know it sounds crazy, but the director warned us to be careful. It seems we do all the spadework and they come along out of nowhere and beat us to the punch. It's happened three times already on major investigations and the big guy is ready to pop his cork."

"What's the problem? Just have one of your tap teams go over the office with debuggers. It should take all of an hour."

"We've had a sweep three times in the last month and we've come up with the big goose egg. Now the boss thinks they're using a Sonimax."

"That's either a Japanese VCR or a sleeping pill."

"Man, you've been away a long time," Clarke said, shaking his head. "They got gizmos in the last year that come right out of *Buck Rogers*. Cameras that can photograph a baseball at over a mile, heat-seeking bullets, night-vision glasses that'd make you swear you're in the middle of a sunny day. We've been hearing about this Sonimax for about three months. Top-secret shit. You aim it like a rifle and it goes through concrete, lead, you name it, and it picks up a whisper at a half mile. You set the dial for four hundred forty feet and ten inches and whatever's within a four-foot radius gets picked up on tape."

"Big Brother's dream."

"You said it, man—and you didn't hear about it from me."

"Thanks for the education. Any problem with the stuff I asked for?"

"Piece of cake, but I can only let you eyeball it. No copies."

"Sure."

Clarke looked around furtively and passed over two folders. As the assistant director, he had access to the huge federal computer in Maryland that supposedly had information on every man, woman, and child in America. I had given him Wackley's Justice Department case number and he got back a copy of his dishonorable discharge proceedings.

Wackley had served in the Marine Corps and had seen action in Vietnam. He was court-martialed for a brawl with an officer and served six months in military prison. There was nothing that seemed terribly important to the Pinto case, except that he was an expert in munitions. Munitions meant explosives, and I remembered that the Porsche bomb was probably a piece of military hardware.

The second folder was marked SUBVERSIVE GROUPS. The NYPD had its own data bank of terror organizations, but it didn't compare with the information the feds had in their computer. There Clarke could access the data by the hammer insignia or the letters. Individual names would also be cross-indexed by the groups they belonged to.

"I see you've got something on them," I said, withdrawing the printouts.

"It's sparse, but interesting. As you can see, they made their appearance out in L.A. a couple of years ago. Until recently we've seen nothing more than a few threatening letters, but lately they've been more active. A bank in Fullerton was knocked over and they claimed credit for it. We nipped an automatic gun deal in the works and the guy we nabbed said he was selling to these Spanish dudes from the ULWC. Their ideology is definitely left-wing all the way; the name comes from the first group Lenin formed back in the Soviet Union, and I'm not talking about the Beatle, either."

"'The United Liberators of the Working Class,'" I read. "It sounds very ambitious."

Clarke smiled. "It's usually a couple of guys and a mimeograph. The more impressive the name, the less impressive the organization."

I knew Matt was right. Yet it was a small renegade outfit like the ULWC that would gain the most by having it known they were responsible for Ned's death. Publicity was the lifeblood of these tinhorn revolutionaries.

If Noolan was one of theirs, he certainly wasn't letting anyone know about it. And why send a quiet letter to Tanya when they could have gotten ink in every paper in the country?

"Thanks, Matt," I said, handing the folders back to him.

"Any help?"

"They raised more questions than answers."

"You want to bat it around? Is there anything I should know?"

"Right now I'm still gathering in all the loose ends. But I know where to find you when the time comes."

Matt picked up his folders and shook hands with me. I thanked him and decided to try Arlene Diamond again.

I called the office number, and the receptionist said that Ms. Diamond wouldn't be in today. I asked if she might be in tomorrow, and the girl didn't know. I asked if Ms. Diamond was out of town, and the girl didn't know. I asked her what she did know, and she told me that Ms. Diamond wouldn't be in today.

I called the home number and it rang six times before it was answered. I know it was six times because I always give the party on the other end seven rings before I hang up. The voice sounded very tired and maybe a bit hung over. "What do you want?" she asked.

"I want to talk to Ms. Diamond," I said.

There was a long pause, so long in fact that I thought I was holding a dead line. I was about to hang up when she said, "Who is this?"

"My name is Resnick. I'm a private detective, and I would like to talk to Ms. Diamond, please."

Again the long pause, but this time I was ready for it. "Does this have anything to do with Bill's death?"

"Yes," I told her.

"Then please come over. Do you have my address?"

It was a house in the exclusive Jamaica Estates section of Queens. I wrote down the number and drove to Queens via the Midtown Tunnel.

I parked the car three houses down and walked the fifty yards to Diamond's place. It was a two-story mansion with white Doric columns that belonged as a backdrop in *Gone with the Wind*. I could have parked in the circular driveway, had it not been for the Lincoln Town Car that blocked it off.

There was a broad bay window on the first floor sealed with expensive-looking drapes, and on the second floor a similar window looked down on the street. The house was nicely framed by twin maples and a well-manicured lawn that was being watered by an underground sprinkler system. I dodged the spray and made it to the front door. It was beautifully carved mahogany with ornate stained glass.

A small decal let me know that the premises were protected by the Sentinel Company. The drawing of a minuteman and his musket would be enough to throw shivers of fear into every hardened criminal I ever knew. A TV camera positioned over the door gave me the once-over as a squawk box asked who I was.

"Slots Resnick," I said, recognizing the voice as the same one I had heard on the phone.

"Please let yourself in. I'll be right down."

A small hallway led into the living room, which wouldn't house all of downtown Newark, but it would be close. There was a baby grand piano near one wall and murals and other paintings on the others. I recognized pieces of Giacometti sculpture and the kind of brightly colored vases that people in movies were always saying "Please don't touch that, it's third-century Ming Dynasty" about. Invariably, Chevy Chase or Steve Martin or Lou Costello would smash the damn thing in the next fifteen minutes.

I sat myself down on a thick sofa, feeling as if I'd sink forever before I hit bottom. It would take a rope and a donkey to pull me out, I thought to myself.

Arlene Diamond walked in just then. She was wearing a pink silk robe with a large script initial *S* over her left breast. The robe was obviously bought during her marriage to Bert, when her name was Sloan.

She was older than I had expected, probably pushing fifty, with very white skin on a sickly thin frame. The deep red lipstick was put on too thick, making her look even paler. Her hair was a wispish reddish-blond color, about medium length. It looked as if she had just gotten up and hadn't looked at herself in the mirror. Her nose had been through a plastic job and was a bit too upturned. Maybe the doctor was the boyfriend Sherry talked about when she described the divorce proceedings.

The very dark sunglasses Arlene wore gave me the initial impression that I was right about the hangover, but she walked rock steady and greeted me with a tired but controlled voice. Another impression that seemed more logical now was that she had been crying. Her demeanor was that of a woman in mourning, perhaps sedated on Valium.

"I'm sorry, I'm just not up to making coffee," she said. "I sent the servants away."

"I'm fine," I told her.

"Mr. Resnick, I think you said you were a private detective?"

"That's right."

"Then someone hired you to investigate Bill's death?"

"No, I was working on another investigation and it crossed over into this one."

"I see."

First reaching up to take off her glasses, she cradled her head in her hands and sobbed. I waited for it to pass, feeling helpless and like an intruder.

"I'm sorry," she finally said, regaining her composure.

"Perhaps another time might be better," I offered.

"No, please stay. I didn't think I would need to talk, but I do. May I ask who hired you? You're not from the studio, are you?"

"No, ma'am. I work for a lady named Carol Simmons. She hired me on another matter."

"I see." Her thoughts were a million miles away.

"Why don't you tell me about Bill," I prodded her gently.

She smiled. "He was the sweetest, most gentle man I ever knew. I can't believe he's dead . . . I just can't believe it. I was sitting in my office and Gina, my secretary, told me that there were police in the building asking questions about Bill. 'What kind of questions,' I asked her. 'Oh, didn't you know,' she said, 'he's been killed.'"

She started crying again. This time I managed to get out of the sofa and walked over to a marble table with a box of tissues on it. I took a handful and gave them to Arlene. She dabbed at her eyes while I found a seat in a leather La-Z-Boy that was more to my liking.

"Did the police question you about your relationship with Bill?"

She shook her head. "No, nobody knew." She looked up and focused on me. "How did you know, Mr. Resnick?"

I told her about finding Bill's body and finding her card in his wallet. I left out the reason I was there and she didn't think of asking.

"Billy wanted to keep it a secret," she explained. "He was Bert's friend and he didn't know how Bert would take it. We were sneaking around like a couple of adulterers. Billy really wanted to tell Bert, but it never seemed to be the right time."

"I'd like to know how you two met," I told her.

She shook her head sadly and I thought she hadn't heard me. I was about to ask the question again when she began talking.

"It seems like a million years ago. We all started Command Studios together in Anaheim. It was Bert and me, Tanya, and poor Ned. Ned had two friends, Billy and Dennis O'Keefe. We were all inseparable in those days. Billy felt bad about how Bert was treating me. He knew about Bert's little girlfriend and he didn't want me to get hurt. He was like that, always very protective."

"You wouldn't have a picture of the group, would you?" I asked her.

"As a matter of fact, I was just looking at one. Just a second."

She came back holding a bunch of photos. She

handed one of them to me. It was a group shot in front of Dodger Stadium.

I took a good long look at Dennis O'Keefe. He fit the bill of the fellow in the front seat of the Seville, but so did half the male population of the country.

"What happened to Dennis?"

"He's in New York with us. He helps around the office and drives me on occasion. Command Studios has the West Coast office with Bert and Tanya, and I take care of the East Coast. Not many people know that I'm a partner in the company, and I prefer to keep it that way. I do public relations and make sure that Bert and Tanya don't throw away everything with their harebrained schemes."

"What schemes?"

"This foolish Crusade for America, or whatever."

"You don't think it's important?"

"Look, Command is in the entertainment business. It should stay out of politics. Bert should know better, but he's so wrapped around Tanya's little finger that he doesn't know what he's doing."

"I got the impression Bert was a superpatriot."

"Puh-lease! He doesn't know anything about the red, white, and blue—the only color he cares about is green, for money. This was all her doing. That Tanya . . . and just look what happened! She lost her husband because of it—not that she cared any."

"She and Ned didn't get along, did they?" I fished.

"The insiders knew about Ned and his fondness for adolescent girls. Billy was his friend and tried to talk to him about it, but Ned wouldn't listen. Bert was scared to death he would get one of them pregnant and that would be the end of the big box office idol. Can you just imagine Bert trying to talk to Ned about messing with kids!"

I tried to bring her back to the subject. "What about Tanya and Ned?"

"Oh, Tanya knew what was going on. Bert told her

to get him straightened out, but there wasn't much she could do. Instead, *she* wound up as Bert's plaything. It's a good thing Ned never found out. He would have killed them both."

"Are you sure about them?"

"Billy told me—Billy knew everything. That's why I believe Tanya killed him." She looked at me for some kind of reaction, but I played it poker-faced.

I thumbed through the rest of the photos. Arlene seemed to have aged twenty years from the time they were taken, which was only about six or seven years ago.

"Did Bill have any enemies?"

"How could anyone be Bill's enemy? He was a big, lovable teddy bear," she said.

I swallowed hard. "Did he ever mention a group called the Union for the Liberation of the Working Class? The ULWC?"

"Billy didn't care about politics, Mr. Resnick," she explained.

"How did he meet Ned?"

Arlene smiled. "Ned hero-worshipped Bill. Bill was everything in real life that Ned tried to be on the screen. Bill and Denny were buddies in the marines. They auditioned for parts together, and at one of the auditions they met Ned. Ned always wanted to know what it was like in the service. He was four-F because of flat feet, or so he claimed. I don't know. Anyway, Ned liked to be around a real hero. Billy won a medal in the marines, you know."

"I didn't know that."

"Oh, yes. For bravery. He was a real hero."

"Would it be too much trouble for you to give me Dennis O'Keefe's address? I'd like to talk to him about Billy too."

"No trouble, Mr. Resnick. No trouble at all."

She found a pencil and wrote down the address. "In fact, Mr. Resnick, would you consider working for me? I'd pay you well to uncover the facts of his murder."

I could have told her to take a number. Instead, I said, "I'm actively working on the case, Ms. Diamond. I can assure you that bringing Billy's murderer to justice is a priority. You've been very helpful to me on that score already."

She nodded. "I loved him very much," she whispered.

"I know you did. I'm sure he felt the same about you."

That started the waterworks going again.

I got up, patted her gently on the shoulder, and made my way to the door.

· ·

15

I got stuck in traffic coming off the East River Drive and across Forty-second Street. I was stopped at the same light where Pinto's limousine had been beached, where Noolan supposedly came up and shot him. It was about the same time of day, too, and I was in the same lane. To make the scene even more eerie, a brown-shirted messenger drove his bike down the center white line, weaving in and out of the lane overspills from both sides.

I shook my head and tried to imagine someone balancing a gun in one hand, hidden by a sling, driving a bike in New York City traffic. The messenger needed both hands, and a whistle to boot, and he was a pro. As I watched him, he fought for his balance twice. It could be done but it wouldn't be easy, I thought.

The bicycle had been nagging at me from the moment I read the reports. Where the hell did it come from? You just didn't find an unattended bike in New York City. People went so far as to remove the front wheel and take it with them whenever they left their bikes.

If Noolan stole it, where was the police report? Ackerman would have loved to show me that Noolan was identified as stealing the bike. It seemed hard to believe that if someone had a bike stolen, it wouldn't be reported.

I made the first left and snuggled the car into a spot in front of a hydrant. I'd need a damn shoehorn to get out. I took two of my business cards and stuck one on the front window, turned the other one over and wrote INVESTIGATION IN PROGRESS. I hoped any NYC foot patrolman would remember my name and give me a free pass. I also took out my empty folded M & M's bag and left it on my windshield. The M & M's bag was a signal to meter maids and the traffic division that this was one of their own, so don't ticket.

There was a phone on the corner and it took me a couple of quarters to get through to the public defender's office and find out that the lawyer put in charge of Noolan's case was Bernice Fleischer. Bernice, or Bunny, as everyone called her, hadn't gone to lunch yet and she had a few moments to talk to me while she was preparing another case. Our paths had crossed over the years and we had always maintained a proper professional relationship. I considered her a liberal, do-gooder, flower child; she looked upon me as being to the right of Attila the Hun.

We exchanged all the remarks one could make about the tragedy of Alex Tucker, and I told her about my interest in the case. I didn't have to be a great detective to discern that Bunny felt Noolan was guilty and she would be going through the motions of a defense.

"Bunny, how about checking the files and telling

me what kind of bike Noolan used on the day Pinto was killed."

"It's a spanking new, ten-speed, powder blue Diamond Back, the Pursuer model, which retails for about four hundred dollars."

"How did you know that so quickly?"

Bunny laughed. "I'm a biking enthusiast. I was trying to figure out a way I could buy the thing after the trial is over. If they auction it, I could pick it up for two hundred."

"Bunny, could Noolan have driven it through New York City traffic with one hand?"

There was a pause while Fleischer considered it. "That's an interesting point, Slots. I never thought about it. This particular bike is very lightweight; it's more for racing than pedaling to and from work. To answer your question, if I was called upon as an expert witness, I would have to say it was certainly possible, but it would be difficult."

"Look Bunny, this case isn't as black-and-white as Ackerman would lead us to believe."

"I don't defend my clients on Ackerman's appraisals," she snapped.

"Okay, okay; I wasn't implying anything, so don't bite my head off. I think it's very strange that there's no report out on a stolen bike worth four bills. I also don't think Noolan had the money to buy a bike like that. So where did it come from?"

"That's another interesting point, Slots, but it really is pure conjecture. There might be a lot of people who for one reason or another wouldn't report a stolen bike. They know the chances of getting something back in this city with our Keystone Kops on the case."

"You're not going to get me upset with that stuff anymore, Bunny. I'm off the force now."

"Yes, I know. I'm going to concede something to you Resnick, but I'll deny it if you ever say I said it."

"What's that?"

"I think you might have been better as commissioner than Mickey Mouse Vargas. At least you have some balls."

"What high praise. My heart, be still!"

"Slots, get me something to sink my teeth into. I wouldn't mind getting some favorable ink for the office, or for myself. Besides, I figure I owe this one to Tuck."

"I'll be in touch," I told her.

I called Carol Simmons and waited for her to scream at the dogs before she finally said hello. "You got me in the middle of feeding them. What's up?"

I gave her some background on the bike her brother was supposed to have used and asked her if he would have had the money to buy a bike like that?"

"Are you crazy? He was borrowing from me and Mildos. He didn't have an extra cent, unless he hit a horse."

For a split second I didn't understand what she meant. I had this mental picture of little Tommy Noolan standing on his tiptoes and punching a horse. "You mean Tommy bet on horses?"

"Pissed me off to no end. I'm giving him four, five bucks a day and he's throwing it away at OTB. It's lucky for him I didn't find out about it till they put him in the slam."

"How'd you find out?"

"They gave me his belongings. I found a bunch of tickets in his wallet."

"You didn't throw them away, did you?" I asked her with my fingers crossed.

"No, they're around here somewhere. Why?"

"Just hold on to them until I can look at them," I told her. "I want you to do something else for me. Do you have any time today?"

"If it'll help Tommy, I'll make time."

I told her what I wanted her to do and made her explain it back to me to be sure she understood.

I was working on the assumption that Tommy Noolan didn't kill Ned Pinto. He may have done everything else that was described in the report Stash handed me, but my gut feeling was he didn't pull the trigger of the gun that killed Ned. If I was wrong about that, everything else was going to collapse like a house of cards.

If Noolan didn't kill Pinto, then the killer had to get the bike from somewhere. If he didn't steal it—which was a pretty good assumption—then he bought it. If he bought it on the day Pinto was killed, he probably bought it at a bicycle store a short distance from the Hyatt. If not, he'd have to travel a long distance on a bike carrying a large gun, which would be spotted by the public. The gun in the sling was a good plan for a short distance in traffic, not for a long haul.

I wanted Carol to canvass all the bicycle stores within a mile radius of the Hyatt and find out if anyone sold a Diamond Back Pursuer on the Saturday morning that Pinto was murdered. If we could match the bike and it turned out the purchaser was someone else, that would throw a crimp in the prosecutor's case.

I told Carol I'd be in my office later in the afternoon and I wished her good luck. She sounded happy that there was something she could do to help.

I walked back toward the Hyatt, stopping to check the car before I continued. I was a winner on two counts, so far. First, the car was still there and not on a hook heading toward the West Side pound. Second, the windshield wipers weren't balancing a fifty-dollar ticket. Not yet, anyway.

I pressed the elevator button and got off on Tanya's floor. It turned out I was about ten minutes late, but that was early in the circles Tanya traveled in. I tapped on the suite door and was greeted by a flunky who asked me what I wanted. Over his shoulder I could see Bert Sloan sitting with two other men on the sofa. He turned and caught my eye before I could speak.

"Dave, let him in," Sloan called, rising and coming to the door. "He's all right Dave, let him in."

Dave moved aside and joined the other two men inside the room.

"Resnick! Shit, man, it's good to see you. Please come in."

Sloan looked tired, the Vegas glitz wearing thin around the edges. The bronze tan looked a little paler, the combed-back hair a bit thinner; even the gold coin around his neck had lost some of its earlier luster. He stared at me with worried eyes. "I'm damn glad you're here," he said solemnly.

"I had a lunch appointment with Tanya."

He nodded. "I know, I know. Just a minute, let me get rid of these guys," he said softly.

He turned to the three business types. "Gentlemen, you're going to have to excuse me. Something has come up that requires my immediate attention."

There was a murmur from the Greek chorus.

Sloan held up his hand. "I give you my word that everything will be taken care of in time for the rally. Please gentlemen, I must ask you to leave." He extended his arms and herded them to the door, all the while mouthing soothing apologies. When he finally got them out he closed the door, locked it, and hurried over to me.

"Mr. Resnick—Slots. Please sit down. I'm going to mix myself a drink. How about you?"

He went to the hidden bar and grabbed the bottle of Dewar's. I told him I could go for a cold one. He made a face but came up with a Heineken from the small fridge.

"You look like shit, Sloan. Where's Tanya?" I said in my usual tactful manner.

He took it in stride. "I feel like shit," he said, handing me my beer and a glass and taking two big gulps of his drink. "I told Tanya to see you last night. She told you everything about the ULWC and about the note?"

I nodded.

He downed the rest of his drink and poured himself another. He was going to get around to what the problem was, but he'd do it in his own sweet time. I put the glass down on the floor and took a swig of the Heiny right from the bottle.

"Tanya jogs in the morning. She cabs to the park and does a jog around the reservoir. She's always jogged in Central Park whenever she's in the city. She left at seven this morning, and she hasn't come back."

He stared at me, waiting for some kind of response.

I killed a few seconds holding the beer up to the sunlight. It looked darker than the Budweiser I was used to, but that could have been the bottle.

"Did you hear me, Slots?"

"I heard you. Why would a woman who received a death threat go for a jog in the park by herself? That doesn't sound too smart."

"She wasn't by herself; she was with Dennis. He was going to jog with her."

"Dennis O'Keefe?"

Sloan looked at me in surprise. "Yes. Do you know Dennis?"

"I know of him. When did you get the note?" I asked.

"Damn! How the hell do you know about that?"

130

Sloan's jaw flapped open like a two-dollar suit-case.

"It's no fun killing someone if you can't gloat about it. Let's see it."

I held out my hand as Sloan went behind the bar. He fiddled for a moment and handed me the letter. It was the same as the one Tanya had shown me last night, except there was a line through her name and EXECUTED written next to it in the same way as was done for Pinto and Wackley.

Sloan was on the edge of panic. "A bellhop brought it up. He said some man gave him a five-dollar bill and told him to bring this up to this suite. He says he can't remember what the man looked like."

Three of the four names had the line and the *Executed* tag. That left only Sloan.

"What should I do, Mr. Resnick? I'm next."

"Call the police," I told him.

He shook his head. "I can't do that. I can't do that to Tanya. This rally is her dream. If I called the po-lice and they tried to shut it down, Tanya would kill me." He winced, probably realizing that Tanya might already be dead. He looked up at me with fire in his eyes. "They are not going to kill this move-ment!" he said angrily. "With Tanya missing, it's even more important to stand up to them."

"I doubt very much that the police would stop the rally at the Forum."

"That's your opinion."

"You think otherwise?"

Although we were the only ones in the room, he leaned over and whispered conspiratorially. "We got confirmation today that the vice president himself will attend. Do you think the Secret Service would let him go on stage knowing there's an armed group of revolutionaries running around killing people?"

Two letters didn't exactly make an armed group of revolutionaries but I didn't comment on Bert's dramatics.

He stood up and started to pace. "No Resnick, we're not going to run away. We'll see this thing through."

"The best of luck to you," I said dully.

I pulled out the wad of hundreds Tanya had left with me last night. "Tanya wanted me to keep this as a retainer. I was supposed to let her know if I was going to take the case."

Sloan eyed the money as I placed it on the coffee table. "You are going to, aren't you?"

"I've been hired by someone else," I told him.

"You don't mean that Simmons woman! Tommy Noolan's sister? You can't be serious, Slots! You're wasting your time."

"That's what I've heard. I never knew people could be so interested in how I spend my time."

"I'll double whatever she's paying you," he said. "Find Tanya, and find these ULWC people. Name your price."

Talk about business trends. All of a sudden everyone was throwing money at me—Sloan, Tanya, Arlene Diamond. The only one who hadn't come up with money in her outstretched fist was the person I was working for: Carol Simmons.

"What about yourself, Sloan? Aren't you concerned about your name being next on the list?"

"I can take care of myself, Slots."

"Sure, everyone can take care of himself. Ned is dead, Wackley is dead, Tanya is missing."

"I can't run away and hide. Someone has to put this thing together. We've got acts coming from all over the country. There are dignitaries to seat, and speeches to schedule. I'm the guy who's got to see it through," he insisted.

"If you had any brains, you'd call in the cops."

"No! No cops. I want you to promise me you won't call the police."

The change in Bert Sloan since the last time I had seen him was extraordinary. The man I saw now was nervous and ill-at-ease. He bore no relation to the self-confident captain of industry I had met the last time I was in the room. Maybe a death threat could do that to you.

"Just what kind of relationship do you have with Tanya?" I asked him.

His eyes narrowed. "What kind of a question is that?"

"A blunt one."

"I don't have to answer that. I don't think it's any of your business."

"If you're serious about my taking the case, it is my business," I told him, matching his dagger stare.

He pointed at me. "You've been talking to Arlene, haven't you? Only someone with Arlene's sick mind would think that Tanya and I would be having an affair. Christ, Resnick! Ned was my best friend."

"It wouldn't be the first time a man bedded his best friend's wife."

"Mr. Resnick, my relationship with Tanya is strictly business." He shook his head. "Damn that bitch! When she finds out about Tanya being missing, she'll throw a party. If Tanya's really been killed, Arlene would stand to make a lot more money from Command Studios."

"How much is a lot?" I asked him.

"The studio's assets aren't completely liquid. We're talking about the prints of movies we own, and the equipment, as well as stocks—"

"Give me a ballpark figure. I don't see any tax men around."

"I would think that each of the three shares are worth close to ten million on paper."

What Bert didn't say was that he, too, stood to

gain financially with Tanya out of the way. "You led me to believe you were a paid flunky for the studio," I told him.

Sloan shrugged. "You wanted me to think you were still employed by the police department. Mr. Resnick, Tanya gave you that money, and Tanya isn't here to take it back. I'm asking you to take this case and get to the bottom of it."

I finished off my beer and leaned back. "Tell me about O'Keefe," I said.

The question seemed to throw him. "What do you want to know about Dennis for?" he asked.

"He was with Tanya, wasn't he?"

"Yes, they often jogged together. Ned hated jogging."

He thought about it. "Denny's just . . . Denny. He was Bill Wackley's friend, and through Bill he was introduced to Ned. He worked in the office here in New York. He really wasn't skilled or anything. Ned made up a job for him. He was like a gofer for the office. He used to chauffeur Arlene around—she doesn't drive—and he worked on the sets, getting coffee, things like that."

"Whose idea was it that he accompany Tanya?"

Sloan shrugged. "I don't know. Tanya's, I guess. Like I said, she liked to jog and so did Dennis. Maybe it was Ned's idea. Before he was killed he said he didn't want her to run alone. What does Dennis have to do with anything?"

"Probably nothing. Like Arlene, though, he knows every one of the people on the list without being on the list himself."

Sloan nodded slowly.

"What kind of a guy is he?"

"Moody, quiet; looks like he's angry. He's a little guy, about five seven, but he can take care of himself. Like Bill, he's an ex-marine. He's one of those guys that seem to be weighing everything you say to him. I never felt comfortable with him around, but Ned liked him. He helped Ned out sometimes."

Something in the way he said that gave me an insight.

"He was the one who procured the teenyboppers for Pinto, wasn't he?"

"What the hell are you talking about?"

"I'm talking about Pinto's appetite for grade-school girls."

"That's just vicious gossip; more of Arlene's lies."

"Don't bullshit me, Sloan. I met two of Ned's kiddie corps myself. A couple of kids up from Shreveport who Ned banged for luck. Don't tell me you didn't know what was going on!"

Bert sighed and made a face. "Okay, okay. I guess it doesn't matter now whether his reputation is protected."

"It must have scared you pretty bad that someone was going to discover Pinto's little vice."

"Sure it did," Sloan said quietly.

"So you got Dennis to quietly bring the girls to Ned."

"Yeah, he arranged things. He made sure they were clean and on the pill."

"Did Tanya know about it?"

"I don't think so. If she did know, she never let on. Look, Slots, you've got to understand about movie stars. I've seen a lot of them. They all have one vice or another. With some it's nose candy, with others it's booze. Some go for boys, girls, or animals, for Christ's sake. I don't condone it, but they're a breed apart. They've got all kinds of pressures, they're exposed to enormous amounts of money—"

"Spare me, Sloan. I'm starting to get weak in the knees."

I had heard that rap about the hard life of movie stars one time too many. If they wanted to know about pressure, let them try to support a family

135

driving a cab in Manhattan. Let them load a cargo ship at five in the morning off a Brooklyn pier with the wind making the chill factor forty below. Where's the pressure in making a million a picture up front with a piece of the gross and a guaranteed income for the rest of your life? Pressure was shooting a game of pool with a couple of toughs for twenty bucks a pop when you only had ten bucks in your pocket.

"You're a cold bastard, aren't you?" Sloan said.

"Liquid nitrogen. Have you called O'Keefe's apartment?"

"Every ten minutes. I even sent a few people to walk around the reservoir. I don't know what to do now."

"Just sit tight. If Tanya's okay, she'll get in touch with you. Don't let anyone in here unless you know who it is."

A couple of minutes later as I rode down in the elevator I remembered I hadn't taken the money. I decided it was because I really didn't want to work for Sloan.

I was feeling pretty good about my cavalier attitude toward money—until I saw the fifty-dollar ticket on my windshield.

16

I checked the address Arlene Diamond had given me and headed west to Ninth Avenue. Dennis O'Keefe lived only fifteen blocks from the Hyatt, but it might as well have been fifteen miles.

The area was laced with porno movies and massage parlors. Marquees vied for attention proclaiming the virtues of their incredible "hot" shows with all-time box office smashes like *Forbidden Ecstasy, Tabu 4, Student Sluts,* and *Freaky Nymphos from Outer Space.* I hoped the academy wouldn't overlook these classics when Oscar time rolled around.

O'Keefe lived in a walk-up fronted by a seedy-looking bodega. Three men in various stages of sobriety sat chatting in Spanish on wooden crates, sipping from beer cans they held in paper bags. *"Policía,"* one of them said as I walked up the stairs.

The phone was ringing in Dennis's apartment: probably Sloan trying again. I knocked but got no response as the phone kept ringing. It looked like a cheap lock and it was fairly low on the door frame. I did my Bruce Lee impression and kicked it a couple of inches below the knob.

You learn in the police academy how easy it is to kick in a lock, even a good lock. At the striking point of the kick there's a fifteen-hundred-pound-per-square-inch force on the lock, which is like having a wrecking ball do the job for you. Ninety percent of all break-ins occur when doors are kicked in. O'Keefe's lock gave it up on the first try.

I wasn't worried about the thud bringing up curious neighbors. In this neighborhood, you minded your own business.

O'Keefe's place was a simple railroad flat with three dingy rooms. The place was a sty and stunk from the open garbage can in the kitchen.

The phone finally stopped as I made my way into the bedroom. The bed had been slept in and was still unmade. There were two overflowing ashtrays on a bureau that doubled as a TV stand, and an old yellowing photograph of a woman with bad teeth wearing a simple print dress. She was standing next to a stern-looking gent with a handlebar mustache. O'Keefe's parents?

The living room held nothing more than a radio and a lumpy chair on top of a circular brown rug that most people would have used in the bathroom. No attempt had been made to furnish the place. It looked more like a transient's room in an SRO.

I went back into the bedroom and opened the drawers and closets. There was a large array of clothes, most of them well kept and expensive. O'Keefe had a couple of Dior suits, which could run up to five hundred apiece. There were Sulka ties and Prince Grinido white-on-white shirts.

There were no other pictures or papers around, and that struck me as strange. Most people had warranties, tax receipts, insurance forms, hospital papers, marriage licenses, letters, bills. Paper was the lifeblood of modern society and O'Keefe didn't have a scrap of it. I looked under the bed and under the bureau for a tin box or portable file: nothing.

There was nothing in the bathroom that would shed any light on O'Keefe either. I checked out the toilet tank and drained it, looking for a piece of string that might let me know that something was hidden in the overflow pipe. Nothing.

I pulled off the back of the radio in the living room, and looked in the cushions of the antique chair. Nothing. Back in the bedroom, I checked the drawers again, patted down the clothes in the closet. Nothing.

I turned the toaster upside down and disrupted a family of roaches on a picnic. Nothing. I pulled a chair over and looked into the bowl of the kitchen light fixture. Something!

I found the papers I was wondering about in an envelope. There were O'Keefe's birth certificate and his Social Security card. There was a later photo of the woman in the snapshot in O'Keefe's bedroom, looking a lot older and wearing a troubled smile. There were also marine discharge papers, and love letters addressed to him and signed "Bill." Bill Wackley? It was certainly a good guess.

I went back to the discharge papers and looked at the unit number. Dennis and Wackley had been stationed together; O'Keefe belonged to Wackley's platoon. The letters had been coming continuously and then abruptly stopped almost a year ago.

There was no need to go too deeply into the letters. From the things said about Command Studios and the references to the marines, Wackley was definitely the man corresponding with Dennis O'Keefe. I put the envelope and its contents back in the fixture.

The phone started to ring again and this time I picked it up. It was Sloan. He sounded disappointed when he found out it was me and that Dennis hadn't returned. There was still no sign of Tanya. He hung up with a worried good-bye.

The modern phone was incongruous in the shabby apartment. Funny how some people didn't care about their physical surroundings but they still had to have the latest high-tech gadgets available. It was one of those slick jobs with speed dialing, a mute button, and redial. Out of curiosity, I pressed Redial to see who O'Keefe had called last.

It rang twice and then a female voice answered. "Pan American Airways, please hold."

I held until she came back on.

"Pan American Airways, how may I help you?"

"Where is your office located?"

"JFK Airport."

I had nothing else to say, but she helped me out.

"Would you like information on our flights to the Virgin Islands?"

"Sure."

"Where did you read our ad?"

"I don't really recall," I told her.

"Okay, flights leave JFK every three hours and land at Harry S Truman Airport, which is just outside of Charlotte Amalie, the capitol of Saint Thomas."

She was about to give me the special rates when I felt the cold steel of a gun being nuzzled under my ear.

"Hang it up, sport," Dennis O'Keefe said menacingly.

I put the receiver down in its cradle and turned around slowly to face O'Keefe. I recognized him from Arlene's picture. He was about five eight, with that greasy black hair that I remembered from my ill-fated ride in the Seville. I could see he knew me, too.

"Nice seeing you again," I said.

He patted me down like a pro, pulled the special

out from my shoulder holster and tossed it on the chair. He was a mean-looking bantam rooster with a pug nose and steel-hard blue eyes. Out of a hundred men, the stereotypes would lead you to believe that he'd be the last one you'd think was gay.

"I could put a bullet into you now, Resnick, and there ain't a jury in the world that would convict me. You broke into my place and I thought you were a burglar."

"Why would you want to do that? We're both working for the same people. I just came in here to make sure you were all right. I was just on the phone with Bert Sloan. He sent me here to check on you. He was worried that something happened to you and Tanya."

He glared at me. He was wearing a blue sweat suit that was stained with perspiration and a matching blue sweatband on his forehead.

"If you're lying, you're a dead man," he said, pulling my hair and pushing me down on the floor. He kicked me away from the phone and punched in two numbers on the speed dialer.

"Sloan? Yeah, it's me. No, I don't know. We were together and then she decided to go to the john. I did a half lap and came back for her but she was gone. . . . I been looking all over for her, for Chrissakes! That's why I just come back now. I don't know. . . . Stop your fuckin' screaming, for Chrissakes! You send Resnick to my place? Yeah, he was pokin' around and he busted my door. Yeah . . . okay, okay. Then you were just on the phone with him? Yeah . . . okay. Yeah . . . I'll let you know."

He tucked his gun into his waistband and I felt a lot better. I stood up slowly.

I'd seen a lot of guys like Dennis O'Keefe. I grew up in Hell's Kitchen with the "shanty Irish" and I knew a dozen guys who probably grew up to be just like Dennis. I got the impression that if Sloan hadn't said the right thing, I would have been in deep trouble.

This was the second time that O'Keefe had me at a disadvantage, and I didn't like it. My side ached where he had kicked me.

I waited for him to put the phone down and turn in my direction. I started my swing from behind my ear, like a quarterback getting set to throw a fifty-yard bomb. I connected flush on O'Keefe's chin and felt the bone-rattling impact right up to my shoulder blade. He spun around like a top and tumbled over the radio, which bounced on the floor and started playing easy-listening music. O'Keefe crashed head first into the wall behind him and sank to the ground as if in slow motion. He was out cold.

I took his piece and went into the kitchen. I filled up a couple of glasses with cold water and came back and poured them on O'Keefe until his eyes fluttered open. He groaned and touched his jaw gently, moving it from side to side. There was a red bruise and some swelling.

"What'd you do that for?" he asked me.

"That's for my ride in the Caddy with you and Bill Wackley," I told him.

"I'm going to kill you, Resnick. I swear on my mother I'm going to kill you!"

"Like you killed Wackley?"

His eyes became narrow slits of hate. "You're crazy! Why would I want to kill Bill? He was my best friend!"

"Why did the two of you decide to rough me up?"

He sneered at me. "Because we didn't want you pulling some shit to get that Noolan creep off. Bill told me you got a lot of connections and you would pull something. We didn't think it was right. Ned was our buddy."

"You ever stop and think that maybe it wasn't Noolan?"

"It's Noolan, all right. He's part of that Commie organization, Bert told me about, the ULWC."

"You rig my car? You and Bill?"

"We didn't do shit. I read about it in the paper and to tell you the truth, I was sorry they missed you."

"What happened to Tanya?"

"Go fuck yourself!"

I asked him a few more questions, but he'd said all he was going to say. He sat rubbing his jaw, looking at me with venom in his steely eyes.

I picked up my gun and holstered it, then tossed Dennis his after removing the bullets. "See you around," I told him as I went to the door.

"You sure as hell will," he said ominously.

The sun was low in the sky, right at the angle where your sun visor does the least good. I wound up squinting my way downtown and by the time I got to my neck of the woods, I had a pounding headache.

I stopped at the twenty-four-hour fruit store on the corner and the brown-skinned man, who could have been from any one of forty Third World countries, assured me that Anacin-3 was the best thing for my headache. He was in this country for a year and a half and already he had mastered pharmacology. He even offered me a glass of water so that I could immediately down his prescribed medication.

I stuck the key in my office door and felt the alarm area in my brain send off Roman candles. I always double-lock my door. It's a habit, and I never forget to do it. I pulled the key out and stepped off to the side. I stood perfectly still and listened intently.

Someone was moving around in the waiting room. Whoever it was hadn't heard me and didn't seem to be making any attempt to be quiet. When I heard the humming, I knew who it was.

I walked in just as Sherry was about to light two candles on the improvised dinner table.

"Oh . . . hi, Slots," she said. "I hope you don't mind that I used the key you gave me, but I wanted to surprise you."

She had put a tablecloth on the waiting room coffee table and had two place settings, complete with cloth napkins and candles in silver holders. There was the smell of warm food coming from two large paper bags and Sherry pulled out plates of pungent lobster, butter sauce, and baked potatoes. There were more goodies from the other bag: wine, breadsticks and rolls, as well as crystal stemware and expensive-looking china.

"What's this all about?" I asked her.

"It's my way of saying I'm sorry," she said sheepishly. "I was kind of hard on you yesterday; you didn't deserve it. You've always been straight with me, and—oh, what's the difference. I felt sorry for you, okay? I figured you could go for a good home-cooked meal."

"You cooked all this?"

She made a face. "Well, not really. There's a place near my office they call The Traveling Feast. I did pay for it, though."

"I think it's just great," I said, pulling up a chair.

"You mad at me?" she asked in a little-girl voice.

"Anything happen between you and that guy?"

"Nah. The more I was with him, the more I realized how much I missed you."

"I missed you, too," I said. I wasn't just mouthing the words. I hadn't realized how important Sherry had become to me.

"Easy, Slots! Don't get too heavy. For a second there, I thought I saw a funny look cross your face."

"Just hunger pangs," I said.

Sherry put the food on the plates and poured the wine. We ate and we talked. She asked me about the case and I found myself babbling away like a kid on his first date. Sherry was interested and asked some pertinent questions.

"What do you think happened to Tanya?"

"I don't think she's dead, if that's what concerns you."

"Why not?"

"She was supposedly abducted from the park. If they wanted to kill her, they would have done it right away. You can't drop a body off in Central Park and a whole day goes by without someone finding it. That means she's being held somewhere else, so there's no sense in worrying about her until the ransom demands come in."

"But Sloan had a paper they sent that says she was executed."

"That's a common ploy. It's a means of pyschologically breaking the people who are closest to the kidnap victim. First they take away hope, then they restore it, then they threaten, then they relent."

"What do they want?"

"If this group really does exist, they'll want money, and they'll want the rally to be called off."

"But Sloan said he won't stop the rally."

"I don't think he will. He believes—and I think he's right—that Tanya would rather die than give in."

We finished the wine, and Sherry put the plates into plastic bags that The Traveling Feast had supplied.

"How do you like the way I do the dishes?" She smiled.

I pulled her onto my lap and she entwined her arms around my neck. "I like it a lot. It gives us time to—"

There was a heavy knock on the office door.

"Mr. Resnick, are you in there?"

I recognized the voice. It was Carol Simmons. I

gave Sherry a look and she shrugged. "Do you want me to leave?" she asked.

I sighed. "No."

I let Carol in. She wasn't alone. The hulking figure of Don Mildos followed her into my office.

Mildos stuck his nose in the air like a dog catching a scent. "I smell lobster . . . I smell lobster," he sing-songed.

Sherry flashed me a what-the-hell-is-this look. I guess she had never seen a two-hundred-and-forty-pound man sashaying around my office wearing huge plaid shorts, a maroon polo shirt with a green tie, black ankle-length socks and shoes, and, of course, a sailor cap.

"Oh, it's all finished," he said, finding the bag of garbage.

"Sorry Dr. Mildos, if we knew you were coming we'd have saved something for you."

"Oh, that's okay." He turned his attention to Sherry. "Hi! I'm Dr. Mildos, Professor of English lit, and you are. . . ?"

"That's Sherry," I said.

She gave an uncomfortable half nod. Mildos extended his hand to shake and when Sherry reluctantly put out hers, Mildos kissed it at the wrist. "Chahmed," he said, with a small bow.

"Sherry, this is Carol Simmons."

Carol was wearing a hot pink tank top over white slacks they used to call Capri pants. She wore spike heels, which accentuated her backside. If you called Central Casting for a hooker, Carol would have filled the bill. The WHAT THE FUCK YOU LOOKIN' AT? button pinned to her top did little to dispel the impression.

"Yeah, how you doin'?" she said impatiently. "Slots, we got to talk!"

"It's okay. Sherry is a friend of mine. She's been helping with the case."

"Oh, yeah? Well, thanks. I feel kind of funny since

I haven't been able to give you guys any money, but I'm expecting something in the mail real soon and as soon as I get it, I'll do the right thing. I want you to know that I appreciate everything you're doing."

"That's okay," I said.

"Well let me tell you what happened!" she said excitedly. "You were right about the bike. I found a place called Roy's Broadway Cycles three blocks from the Hyatt, and they had a sales slip for a powder blue Diamond Back Pursuer sold on the same Saturday that Ned Pinto was killed. That bike cost over three bills! There was no way my brother could even dream about having three bills!"

"Did you try all the other stores?" I asked her.

"Yep. Me and Don have been out since you called. We must have tried ten or fifteen of them."

"Did Roy's remember what the person who bought the bike looked like?"

Carol shook her head sadly. "No, all they had was the sales receipt. The man who sold it said he sells bikes all day long and he wouldn't remember if his mother bought the bike."

"Damn!"

"Doesn't that help though, Slots?" Sherry asked. "Where would Tommy get that kind of money? He couldn't possibly have bought that bike."

"The district attorney will say that it wasn't necessary for him to buy it—all he had to do was steal it from the person who did. I was hoping the salesman would have been able to tell us something about the customer. That way we might have gotten a lead to follow."

I could see that Carol was upset. She sat down, seeming to sag in the chair. I gave her a reassuring look and she managed a half smile.

"What about the tickets from the Off Track Betting parlor?" I asked her. "Did you bring them?"

"Don has them," she said. "What in the world would you want them for?"

Mildos giggled. "Maybe he figures he'll find a winning ticket and that will pay his fee." He handed me about twenty of the thin strips of paper.

"You're a mental case, Mildos," Carol said disgustedly.

"You're right, but that doesn't mean I'm not a nice person," Mildos responded cheerfully.

I went through them, not actually thinking I had a chance to find what I was looking for, but nevertheless . . . there it was! I checked twice, and then another time, to be sure I was reading the ticket correctly.

"These were taken from Tommy's wallet, right? They're definitely Tommy's?"

"Slots, what is it?" Sherry asked.

"Yeah, Tommy liked to save them," Carol said. "What about it?"

I held the ticket in the air. *This* is something we can use!" I told them. "Come here and I'll show you something." I waited for them to gather around and then I placed the ticket on the table. "Over here you have the date. What does it say, Carol?"

"May twenty-fourth," she read. "Hey! That's when it happened."

"Right! Now look in this corner. Do you see a bunch of numbers strung together? The first three correspond to the branch number where the ticket was bought: that's one three four, which would be the OTB around the corner from your house. I noticed it when I met you the first time. The second two numbers, oh six, tell us what window sold the ticket. And the third set of numbers, one one five oh, relate to what?"

"The time!" Sherry exclaimed.

"Right! Pinto was killed at twelve ten. There's no

way that Tommy could have bought this ticket, got on a train, stolen a bike, and then killed Pinto."

"He must have snuck away to make a bet while I was talking to Don. But I know he was in the chair sunning himself when the bulletin came on about Pinto being shot."

"This means Thomas is in the clear," Mildos added.

"Hold on, everybody. This is just a start. It really doesn't mean much of anything. All we have is a ticket that shows the owner purchased it in Brooklyn about a half hour before Ned's death. Now we've got to establish that it was Tommy who bought the ticket."

"I'll go over there now. I can find the person at window six and ask about Tommy," Carol offered.

"No, they're probably closed by now, and it's a better idea to find out the name of the ticket seller before asking questions. We don't want to take a chance of scaring someone off. The person on the window now may not be the same person who worked the morning of the twenty-fourth."

"Well, how do we find that out, Slots?" Sherry asked.

"We'll call the public defender's office and have them send over an investigator."

I picked up the phone and gave Bunny Fleischer a call. She listened to what I had to say and managed to offer up a small amount of enthusiasm as she copied down the information. "This might mean something, Slots, if we can get someone at the OTB branch to confirm Noolan's being there." She assured me she'd put one of her best people on it.

"Now what?" Carol wanted to know. "I hate just sitting around not being able to do anything. At least today I felt I was useful."

I assured her that she and Mildos had been a terrific help.

"All right, Simmons. I am starved! Let's stop the
gabbing and wolf down some food."

"You're always starved, Mildos." Carol shook her
head. "Whattaya say, Resnick? You got anything
else for us?"

"Just go home. As soon as something breaks, I'll
let you know."

Mildos was already at the door. "You heard the
man. Let's go!"

Sherry waited until they left and then shook her
head. "Wow! What a couple of characters!"

"I know. I'm sure I'm now going to hear about the
benefits of being head honcho of Pit Stops Incorpo-
rated."

"Nope; no lectures today. I'm turning over a new
leaf. Do what you want, no arguments from me."

I looked at her quizzically. "What's going on?"

"A strong dose of reality. If I make you over into
my image of you—even if you'd allow it—you
wouldn't be happy. You'd resent me and feel I talked
you into something. I don't know if I could stand
that responsibility. I know it would destroy us—and
damn it! I missed you."

"Sherry, I—"

"You don't have to say anything, Slots. Maybe I'm
the one that has to change. Could you use a partner?" she asked, smiling.

"You better stay where you are. One of us has to
earn a living, and somehow I don't have that much
confidence in whatever it is that Carol is 'expecting
in the mail.'"

I went and held her in my arms. She kissed me,
and I breathed in the scent of roses and lilacs.

We made love as if we hadn't been together for
years. Mouths, tongues, arms, breasts, thighs, legs

met, probed, held, squeezed, rubbed, entwined at the right times . . . with the right results.

Afterward, with her sleeping soundly in my arms on the convertible sofa, I thought about what Sherry had said. It hadn't been easy for her to sweep away her strong feelings about commitment and plans. Her accepting, even for the moment, the relationship on my terms made me feel uneasy. What was it she had said? She wouldn't want to force me to live the life she wanted for me, because in the end she knew I would resent it—and her. Did I want her to accept my no-strings life-style? Shouldn't I be concerned that after a while she'd resent me?

I remembered how I felt knowing she had invited another man to her home for dinner. Thought you were too secure to let something like that bother you, right, Slots? Pretend it's not driving you crazy not to ask her if anything happened between her and that creep from the office.

Who said he's a creep? He might very well be a heck of a nice guy.

Besides, you know nothing happened. Sherry told you that the more she was with him, the more she thought about you.

Yeah, but when did she start thinking about me?

Slots, look at you, you're jealous!

Get out of here, I'm not jealous. No way!

Sherry woke up with a start. She looked up at me. "What's the matter," she said sleepily.

"Nothing. Go back to sleep."

"Mmm." She curled up beside me with her head on my chest.

"Sherry, did you fool around with that guy you had at your place?"

"Uh-uh."

I pulled her even closer to me and closed my eyes. It felt as if she belonged there.

. . . .

17

I was waiting at the front of Roy's Broadway Cycles at the steel gates that covered the long
storefront window and door. The gates had become part of the landscape of New York after
the riots of the sixties, when a small group of under-
privileged youths underscored their plight by breaking store windows and stealing TVs and liquor. This
inspired protest, ranking several notches under
Gandhi's efforts against the British, did accomplish
several things: store owners who stayed in poor
neighborhoods now paid higher insurance rates, put
in alarms, brought in security guards, and shelled
out money for these steel gates. All of these costs
were passed on to the consumers, who were still un-
derprivileged and became even more so when the
price of goods became significantly higher.

As a beneficial aspect of the gate installations, a
group of con artists, dubbed the five-bucks-a-week
boys, were put out of business. These characters
called themselves a protection agency against win-
dow-breaking vandals. For five bucks a week they'd

make sure no one broke your store window. If you didn't pay them, they'd break the window night after night until you did. The five-a-week boys had their own routes and territories staked out, but occasionally a hapless store owner might be paying two or three protection agencies not to break his windows. The steel gates put an end to that lucrative business.

I decided the man coming down the street was Roy. First of all, he was riding a bicycle, which was a pretty good hint. And he had this outdoor, back-to-nature look, with khaki shorts, white cotton shirt, and sandals.

"Hi there. Looking for a bike today?" he asked, getting off his Avanti and taking a swig from a plastic bottle he pulled out of a backpack. He was in his fifties, with a Hawaiian tan, long gray hair, and a well-cared-for snow white beard.

"Not today. I'd really like to ask you a few questions."

"Sure, happy to answer them, if I can. Would you mind waiting until I get the gate up?" he asked, pulling a set of keys from the backpack.

"No problem; I'll give you a hand."

"I've got this kid who's supposed to be here by now, and he's supposed to lift the gate, but he's constantly late and I always end up doing it myself," he said.

"Why don't you fire him?" I got my end of the gate up and waited for Roy to lock it in place. He opened the door and turned off the alarm.

"I'd like to, but it'd take me too long to replace him. I had the sign out three and a half weeks before he came along. Nobody wants minimum-wage jobs today, except old people. I can't have some sixty-five-year-old codger lifting up packages and carrying them to people's cars. Every kid today wants to start out at the top. Nobody ever heard of entry level.

What the hell, a kid can make more selling crack in an afternoon than I can pay him in a month. I'm Roy Blanchard; nice to meet you." He stuck out his hand.

"Slots Resnick."

"What do you want to know about bikes, Mr. Resnick?"

"It's not bikes I want to ask you about."

"Oh?"

"I'm a private detective, and I'm investigating a homicide. I have reason to believe the killer used a bike that was purchased here."

"I had two other people come in here yesterday—"

"Yes, I know, they were canvassing different bike stores."

Blanchard covered his mouth and chuckled. "I'm sorry; they were such a funny couple. The heavy fellow sat himself down on a child's bike and then he couldn't get out of it. He walked over to the woman with the handlebars stuck on his stomach and the seat wedged to his can. Two of us had to pull it off him." He laughed again at the memory. "I swear to God, I thought it was a 'Candid Camera' bit."

I smiled with him. "Well, it's like you said, Roy: good help isn't easy to find."

"I went poking through my receipts, like they asked me, and any second I thought I'd see that . . . what's his name?"

"Alan Funt."

"Right. I'm waiting for Funt to come walking in telling me to look into an umbrella or something that's really a camera."

"Yeah, well, maybe another time. Look, that sales slip that you came up with from the twenty-fourth: would you mind if I had a look at it?"

Roy thought for a moment. "Yeah, I think I pulled it out and left it in the desk drawer."

He went over to the desk near the register and

opened the drawer. "Right, here it is: Saturday, May twenty-fourth."

I read the receipt. It was for a powder blue Diamond Back costing three hundred seventy-five dollars. The customer paid cash. Next to the salesman's name, Carlos, was the model and serial number.

"Can I use your phone?" I asked Roy.

"Sure, if it's a local call."

I called Bunny Fleischer and read the serial number of the bike off to her and asked her to check it for a match. She said she'd look it up and call me back.

I hung up the phone and went back over to Roy, who was working on the pedal of an old-looking Royce.

"Would you hand me that oilcan over there?" he asked, pointing to a can of Magic Marvel. "Be careful not to get yourself dirty."

I gave it to him and watched him work for a few minutes. "This salesman, Carlos; do you think he might remember who he sold the bike to?" I asked.

"Carlos can't remember anything. It's a wonder he can find his way here every day. I think your friends talked to him and all they got were shrugs."

Roy picked up a screwdriver and used it to stretch the chain.

I thought of a different approach. "Any way of telling whether the bike was sold early or late in the day from the receipt number?"

"How could that help you?" Roy wanted to know. He turned the bike over and, using the pedal, spun the wheel. The action was smooth, with a metered tick on each revolution.

"I'm trying to show that the guy who's accused couldn't be in two places at the same time."

Roy exhaled slowly. "Well, I'm afraid the receipt book won't be much help. Y'see, I got four men on

1 5 5

the floor, and all they do is pick up a book—any book—and write orders. No way that number could help."

The phone rang and Roy went to get it. From his conversation I could tell it was Bunny. He handed me the phone.

"Yeah?"

"They match. Where'd you get the numbers from?"

"I'm at the bike store where it was purchased on the Saturday that Pinto was killed," I told her.

"Did you get an ID on the purchaser? Was it Noolan?"

"I haven't talked to the salesman, but I don't think he'll remember anything."

"Shit!" Bunny said in a most unladylike way. "Back to square one," she said sadly.

"Excuse me," Roy interrupted.

"Hold on, Bunny."

"Did I hear you say Saturday?" Roy asked.

"Yeah, Saturday the twenty-fourth."

"Well, I can help you a little bit then," Roy said, wiping his hands on a gray towel. "You see, one of our salesmen, Abe, had a son getting bar mitzvahed. I closed down that morning in order for the staff to be able to attend services in Abe's shul. We didn't get back here until twelve, so whoever bought that bike had to buy it after midday."

"Bunny, did you get that!" I couldn't keep the excitement from creeping into my voice.

"That means if we—"

"Right! If we can establish that Tommy bought the ticket at eleven fifty, he couldn't have bought the bike and shot Pinto at twelve ten."

There was a short pause on the other end. "I'll get back to you, Slots. Where can I reach you?"

"Give me a call at my office in about an hour," I told her.

I hung up and thanked Roy again.

"I'm glad to help. I'm a big mystery fan, y'know. I've been reading mystery books since I was a kid."

"The books are a lot different than the real cases," I told him. "In real life, the heroes also die."

"Yeah, I guess that's true."

I shook his hand and assured him that if I ever needed a bike, he'd be the man I'd see.

"Beats a car," he said.

"Tell me about it!"

I called Sloan as soon as I got into the office to see if there was anything new on Tanya.

"No, damn it! It's as if she just fell off the earth," Sloan said nervously. "Tomorrow's the rally, and I'm supposed to be in fifteen different places at once, and all I'm doing is monitoring the phone."

"Call me if anything happens," I told him.

"Yeah, sure."

Now it was my turn to monitor the phone. I was hoping Bunny would call me with the information that would spring Tommy Noolan. As usual, the telephone didn't ring while it was being watched.

I walked away from it and went into the waiting room. I thumbed through a magazine, and made a big production out of changing one of the light bulbs in the modern-looking long-necked lamp. Then I went back into my office, walked around the desk twice, and plopped myself down in the chair.

Naturally, as soon as I got comfortable, the phone rang.

"You're a genius!" Bunny Fleischer said.

"Tell me what happened."

"I went down to OTB myself and saw the manager of the branch, who looked up his records for the twenty-fourth. It seems they hire extra people for Saturdays, since that's their busiest day. The fellow who was on window six on the twenty-fourth was a part-timer named Horace Fields."

"Did he remember Tommy?"

"Well, he wasn't in today. I had to call him at home, and luckily, he was there. Yes, he did remember Noolan. It seems that he's a veteran also and he remembered a fellow coming in and striking up a conversation with him. The reason he specifically remembered Tommy was because Noolan went into a long diatribe against Agent Orange. Fields had been suffering from headaches, and Noolan recommended a doctor who was a specialist in treating Vietnam vets who'd been exposed to the defoliant. Fields didn't know if he had been exposed, or if his headaches had anything to do with it, but he did go to the doctor Noolan recommended and he's been feeling better."

"Was he sure it was Noolan?" I asked.

"I went to his home and showed him Tommy's picture. He gave a positive ID. Not only that, Slots, but how's this for the pièce de résistance: he even had the matchbook that Tommy wrote the doctor's name and address on. I happened to have some papers that Tommy had signed for me, and I'm sure the handwriting matches."

"Where the hell has this guy been?"

"He's not interested in the news. He likes to read and listen to music in his spare time. He didn't even know who Ned Pinto was," Bunny said incredulously.

"Well, thank God for Mr. Fields's headaches."

"Damn right! Y'know Slots, a case like this can make careers."

"Or break them," I said, thinking of Ackerman.

"I don't have to tell you, do I, how important it is that you keep quiet about all this."

"In other words, you want to leak it to the papers yourself."

"That's not what I want to—"

"It's okay. I just want to tell Noolan's sister. She's been the one in his corner all along and I've got to let her in on the good news."

"Okay, but tell her to keep it quiet," Fleischer warned.

"She will. She doesn't want anything to jeopardize her brother."

"Uh, Slots, I'm really not too good at saying thanks. . . ."

"You don't have to: you were willing to listen; you made an effort. Tuck would have been impressed," I told her.

"Yeah . . . you're pretty impressive yourself," she said.

I hung up and allowed myself a few minutes to slap some Muenster cheese on a couple of slices of pumpernickel from the minifridge I kept in the office closet. I pulled out a beer and spent five minutes looking for the bottle opener before I found it in the desk drawer, which was the first place I had looked. Some detective.

I tried Carol Simmons's number and got no answer. On a lark, I looked up Mildos in the book and got the same result. Then I called Sherry and filled her in on what Bunny had discovered. She was happy and interested, and we wound up talking about the case for at least ten minutes.

"What about Tanya? Has she turned up?" Sherry asked.

"No. I spoke to Sloan, not long ago and he hadn't heard from her."

"Are you going to find her, Slots?" she asked me.

"It's not my case. I couldn't get involved until I finished proving Noolan's innocence. I told Sloan he should call the police. He doesn't want to, because he's afraid they'll change the Vice President's plans and he won't come to the rally."

"But Tanya's life may be in danger."

"We don't know that, Sherry. For all we know, the whole kidnapping scenario could be a publicity stunt."

"Do you think so?"

"No," I admitted.

The banging on the door caught my attention. "Got to go, Sherry," I told her, "someone's at the door."

The someone was Bert Sloan. I let him in and he fell on the waiting room couch.

"I need a drink, Slots. Do you have anything?" He seemed almost desperate.

"Relax, I'll be right back.

It wasn't a big-deal bar, just a shelf next to the fridge with a half dozen glasses, a bottle of Scotch, and a bottle of vodka. I poured the Scotch and tossed an ice cube in the glass.

"What happened?" I asked him as I handed him the amber liquid.

He swallowed the drink in two gulps.

"Do you have a VCR? They just gave me their demands. It came to the door via Federal Express."

He took a videotape out of his raincoat pocket and followed me into the main office. He waited impatiently while I set up the tape. If he had given the package to the police, they would have dusted for prints and run the tape through the police lab.

It was a mistake for Sloan to have handled the thing, but it made no sense to say anything now.

The tape was the standard VHS type and looked as if it had been recently purchased. I pressed the Play button. The TV screen filled with Tanya's pretty face. She was gagged, and she stared stonily into the camera. Whoever was holding the camcorder panned back, and now Tanya could be seen sitting in a wooden dining room chair, ropes around each wrist tying her arms to the arms of the chair. She was wearing a sweat suit, presumably the same one she was wearing when she had been snatched yesterday morning.

Now the camera panned over the room and settled on a hooded man sitting behind a desk. The room was small, and it looked like it might have been in a hotel. The desk was nondescript and cheaply made. There was a red flag with a hammer and sickle draped on the wall behind the man. A Bulova wall clock was to the left of the flag, the hands pointing to almost 5:30.

The man began speaking—reading, actually, from several sheets of paper. He held them in his black-gloved hand, occasionally pointing and slamming his fist for emphasis. At first I thought something was wrong with the sound; then I realized the voice had been distorted by helium.

It was basically a propaganda exercise: everything that had gone wrong in the last twenty years was the fault of the United States government; the workers were exploited and starving; the elderly were being murdered because they couldn't produce quickly enough to satisfy their capitalist warmongering bosses; the imperialist United States and its gang of stooges were trying to enslave the world and to impoverish the noble workers of the Third World countries. Only a revolution, where the gangster capitalists were overthrown and destroyed, could save America.

The diatribe went on another two minutes before the man in the hood decided to talk about Tanya. It seemed the Revolutionary People's Court had sentenced Tanya, her husband, and others to death. In Tanya's case, however, they were willing to make a deal. If the warmongering Fascists would call off the inflammatory rally for America, Tanya would be released. If the rally went on as scheduled, her execution would be carried out.

The man in the hood stared as the camera moved in for a close-up. The hood had slits cut out where his eyes were, but he had been smart enough to wear sunglasses underneath to disguise his pupils. The tape ended with a shot of Tanya shaking her head defiantly.

I shut the tape off and rewound it.

"Will you help, Slots?" Sloan asked.

"What do you intend to do? Will you call off the rally?"

"No."

"Will you go to the police?"

"No."

"You realize that you're putting Tanya's life in jeopardy."

"I don't need you to tell me that," Sloan snapped. "You saw her, Slots. You know how important this is to her. I know Tanya. She'd rather die than give in to those Red bastards!"

I thought about it. "Now they're taking credit for killing Pinto," I said.

"Sure they did it. If they sweat that kid Noolan long enough, they'll find out he's really a dyed-in-the-wool Red, and part of that gang."

"Noolan didn't kill Pinto. He couldn't have." I told him about the new evidence. Bunny had called all the papers by now.

"But I saw him do it!" Sloan insisted. "I saw him on the bike."

"You saw someone who looked like Noolan, but it wasn't Tommy."

"It was the same gun . . . the same clothes—"

"Tommy was the gunman who shot J. J. Mitchell and made an attempt on Pinto at the hotel. I think Noolan must have taken off his vest and wrapped it around the gun. He probably hid it in the hotel somewhere, figuring he'd come back another time to pick it up."

"You mean someone from the ULWC found it and used it on Pinto?" He shook his head. "I could have sworn it was Noolan."

"You were supposed to think that. The person had the same build, the same color hair, he used the same gun and the same clothes. Everything happened so fast, and with Pinto being shot right next to you, it was easy to see how you could make the wrong identification."

"But, Lieutenant Boddiker—"

"He saw it the same way you did. He was even farther away from the action; he had even less of a chance to make a positive ID. Mitchell was shot, and that was his responsibility. Now Pinto got shot with him sitting right there in the car. I'm sure he convinced himself that the murderer was Tommy."

Sloan looked shaken. "My God! I'm so sorry."

"I wouldn't feel too bad about it. Noolan wanted to do the job. He climbed on the bandwagon when someone else did it for him. Until receiving this tape, it would seem that the real killers were happy to let Noolan take the fall. There are a few things I still can't figure, though. If the ULWC did kill Ned, you'd think they'd want the world to know about it, instead of letting the cops pin it on Noolan. They weren't getting any publicity mileage out of his death."

"What are you getting at?"

"I'm not sure, but it was pretty interesting that someone from the ULWC just happened to be around to find Tommy's gun."

"Sure, unless Tommy was one of them. I've thought that all along. He might have gotten the assignment to kill Ned, and when he botched it up, he let someone else do it."

"Maybe," I said. "But I also can't figure out Wackley's death. Why was Wackley on their hit list? You, Tanya, Ned—you're all principals in Command

Studios. Command Studios is a warmongering outfit in their minds, so you people are sentenced for execution. But why old working-class Wackley?"

"Because Wackley was Ned's best friend."

"So was O'Keefe, but he wasn't put on any list," I replied.

Sloan shrugged.

I decided to throw him a fastball right over the plate. "Your ex-wife thinks that Tanya might have been behind Wackely's death."

"What! Good Lord, man, you can't listen to that bitch!"

"I understand she was very close to Wackley."

"Come off it, Resnick: they were having an affair. I knew about it."

"Did Denny?"

"Denny O'Keefe? I don't know . . . I suppose so. They tried to be cool, but all you had to do was look at them and you could tell. Why? What did it matter if Denny knew?"

"Just curious. He might have felt a little left out. You, Tanya, and Arlene were full partners, and then if Wackley married Arlene, everybody would have a piece of the action except him."

"That's ridiculous. Arlene wouldn't have married Bill. She was a user, Resnick. Today it could be Wackley, tomorrow someone else. She shopped for men like other women shop for shoes," he said bitterly.

"Funny, she seemed to feel the same about you. What about you and Tanya?" I asked him. "You still going to deny your involvement?"

He looked at me for a long second and then he sighed. "I was going to deny it, but now I'm going to tell you the truth." He closed his eyes and leaned his head back on the chair. "Pinto was a sick bastard," he said. "He liked young girls, the younger the better. I'm not just talking eighteen or seventeen, I'm talking twelve and thirteen. There were two or three close scrapes. There was a kid in Houston who was fourteen, and her father came looking for Ned with a shotgun. There was another time in L.A., when he knocked up a black girl who couldn't have been more than twelve. We bought off her mother with ten grand and a job in our California office. There was one kid who hemorrhaged so badly she had to be taken to the hospital.

"He couldn't control his urges, you understand. It was like dealing with an alcoholic. You'd turn around and Ned would be in a closet or behind a tree with some teenybopper. The public knew him as the Iron Man; Chicken Hawk would have been more accurate."

"You covered it up pretty well."

"Bill and Dennis were Ned's friends. They were constantly trying to steer him clear of trouble. We even hired baby-faced call girls that we knew were safe and clean. We all tried to keep it from Tanya, but after a while she found out about it. She had to. Ned was that blatant.

"She came to me crying one night when Ned hadn't come back from a TV spot. She felt completely worthless as a woman. Maybe she needed to prove her femininity. That was the first time. We tried to stay away from one another, but from then on it got easier and easier. Bill knew about us, and he understood. He must have told Arlene."

"Do you think he would have told Pinto?"

Sloan shook his head. "No. And you know what? I don't think Ned would have cared if he did know. Anyway, he never said a word to either me or Tanya. I'll tell you something else, Resnick, something that really gets me sick! If these Commie bastards make good their threat about killing Tanya and me, the one person in the world who'd benefit the most out of it is Arlene. She'd get my cut, Tanya's, and the whole ball of wax would belong to her!"

"If you don't go to the police and Tanya is killed, it's going to look like you let her die so you could have her share," I told him.

"I know it will; that's why I want you to find her for me and get her back."

He took out the money I had left in his office. It was the same three thousand rolled up in a rubber band. He pulled out another wad. "You've got three there, and I'll match it. That's six up front. There's another ten coming to you if you can get Tanya back alive," he told me.

Carol Simmons' money was "in the mail." I'd gotten into the habit of eating, and I liked it. This time I put the money in my pocket. "I'll look into it," I told him.

He seemed to breathe a sigh of relief.

"Your ten grand might be safe, Sloan," I told him. "These people look like professionals. I can't make any promises."

"Just give it your best shot, Slots."

I reached into the desk and pulled out a couple of items. One was a telephone pager, which I would carry on my person. I gave Bert the access number and told him that if the kidnappers contacted him, he was to get in touch with me through the "leash" the minute it happened. The other bit of gadgetry was a tape recorder with a special telephone hookup attached to the mouthpiece by a suction cup. "If they call you on the phone, just press Record and this thing will pick up what they say and tape it."

"Okay, Slots. Thanks." Sloan seemed a lot more confident now. I wished I could be. "What will you do now?" he asked.

"I'm going to take the videotape and have it analyzed. You go on back to your suite and go about your business as usual."

"Do you think I'm doing the wrong thing, Slots?" He looked at me with apprehension, as if afraid of what I might say.

"Even if you called off the rally, who's to say that they'd really release Tanya? You're dealing with fanatics. There's no right or wrong with them. Follow your instincts and hope for the best."

Sloan nodded. "I just have to keep remembering that this is the way Tanya would want it. You could even see it in her face on the tape." He sounded like he was more interested in persuading himself than me.

. . . .

18

I t was four P.M. when I got to the studios of All Alain's Art on Fourteenth.

The high-tech explosion made it possible for independent sound studios to produce records and tapes of a quality that equaled what the big recording studios like Columbia and Atlantic could do.

The Frenchman, Alain Gellet (pronounced Jill-ay), had done a couple of sound analysis jobs for the department back when I was a beat patrolman. We had lost track of each other for a while, and then I was pleased to be invited to the opening of his studio. It had seemed an impossible dream back then, to compete with the major record houses, but Alain had accomplished it. Not only did he have state-of-the-art equipment, but his ear was reputed to be the best in the business.

As we renewed our friendship, he regaled me with stories about the biggest rock stars and how they would record their songs only at the Triple A studio. It had gotten to the point that Alain didn't even know how much to charge.

"To tell you tze truth, Zlots, eef I don' charge too much, zey are disappointed, *n'est-ce pas?* Zey love to complain how I charged zem two, three, five thousand an hour—but zen zey say, 'Ahh, but Alain iss worth every penny.' I think zey like to brag zat zey were charged more zan anyone else."

I climbed the steps to his second-floor studio and waited for him to open the door. His smile went from earphone to earphone when he saw me.

"Ahh, Zlots. Please, come in, come in."

He led me past the small reception room into the glass-enclosed soundproof recording studio. There were huge machines with blinking lights and reels and analog numbers, as well as digital instruments. I recognized an IBM computer; all the rest looked like it belonged in a science fiction movie.

"This stuff come out of a spaceship?" I asked him.

Alain laughed. "Not quite, *mon ami,* but one must keep up with technology, *non?*"

"But of course," I agreed.

"But of course," he repeated.

He took off the headphones and turned a switch on a nearby console. "Now, what ees it I may do for you? You weesh to cut some wax, Monsieur Zlots, and become a punk star?"

"Not quite. I need some help with this." I handed him the videotape. "A lady has been kidnapped, and I was hoping you could put this under your microscope and see if you can pick up anything that might give me a shot at getting her back."

The Frenchman nodded and stuck the tape into what looked like a rewinding machine. "How long do we have, Zlots?" he asked. His usually smiling face now revealed some trouble lines.

"ASAP, I'm afraid. I know how busy you are and—"

"No, no. Nevair too busy for a friend," he said, taking the tape from the machine and giving it back to me. He pulled a much smaller, audio-size tape from another compartment of the mechanism. "You can take zat back. I don' want to zee it, because sometimes tze visual distorts tze accoustical. I just want to zee everything with tze ear."

He took the smaller tape and placed it in something that looked like a tape recorder, but was much larger. In two seconds, the tape ejected.

"It came out," I told him.

"It has fineeshed its work." He walked back and forth from one machine to the next, adjusting dials and turning switches.

He was long and lean, with prematurely gray hair on a narrow, handsome face. He reminded me of a mad scientist, and the white lab coat he wore did nothing to dispel that image.

"Ah, Zlots, do you know what I am doing?"

"I haven't the faintest. Of course, you're talking to a guy who couldn't tell a woofer from a tweeter if they came up and bit him."

"I will eggzplain. You know, when we make records today, we do eet in layers, *n'est pas?* Tzere is tze zinger, zen tze backup, zen each instrument. Each can be recorded zeparately, and we call tzese layers 'tracks.' We can make adjustments through an equalizer and other methods, and in ze end we build a record. It ees like putting together an onion by adding layer after layer. Now, with zees tape you 'ave given me, I will take tze whole onion and I weel peel off one layer at a time. Every different sound recorded will be a layer, or a track. Zen we will amplify each of ze tracks, use a filter, and as you put, put eet under a microscope, eh?"

"How many tracks are there?"

"I weel find tzat out right now with ze computer."

I watched as he punched in some commands. A graph appeared on the screen with hundreds of swirly lines.

"Umm, zees tape is five minutes and nine seconds

and zere are three hundred and forty-seven distinct sounds zat have been recorded. Tze longest of zese is total of three minutes and eight seconds; ze shortest of zese lasts less tzan one fiftieth of a second."

He punched more commands into the computer.

"Now we will eliminate any zound tzat cannot be heard by ze human ear, and zounds which are of too brief a duration. Ah, now we have only two hundred and nine tracks to analyze."

"It sounds like an impossible job," I told him.

"You are right. Zat's why it will take me perhaps ten or twelve hours. I am zorry, my friend, but it cannot be done zooner."

"At four thousand an hour, that means I owe you forty or fifty grand."

"*Oui*, but for compensation I weel accept a ticket and your company at a baseball game zees summer. Deal?"

"Deal."

I stopped at a phone and gave Sloan a ring. He jumped at it before the first ring had completed.

"Anything?" I asked him.

"No. I just did an interview on the evening news. If they watch it, they're going to know that the rally is going on as planned."

"Okay. That means they have to make a decision either to negotiate for something else or carry out their threat. Hang in there," I told him.

I tried Carol Simmons; there was still no answer. That left me with a quarter in my hand, and I used it to try Sherry. She wanted to know about Tanya and I told her what had been happening.

"Do you think they'll really kill her?" she asked.

"I don't think so. They want something, or they would have killed her before. If they can't get the rally stopped, they'll make a pitch for something else—but that's a judgment based on an assumption that these people make rational decisions. There's no way to know if that's true."

There was a three-beat pause. "It's so horrible, isn't it?" she finally said.

"That's why there are people like me to make it right. Call me Mr. Modest."

"I guess that's true, isn't it? I never thought of your job like that before."

"I think I'm softening you up," I told her.

The guy on the radio was talking about fog. It seemed that there was a low pressure system clashing with a high pressure system, and the arctic air currents were meshing with the Gulf Stream to produce barometric conditions, blah, blah, blah. The bottom line was it was going to be a foggy evening in old New York.

The news anchor guy fished for a laugh with "How foggy was it," and the weather guy left him up the creek without a punch line when he said, "Foggy enough to cause some accidents in the outlying suburbs, Stan." Stan coughed a couple of times and went on to give the headlines. That's why anchor guys made three times as much as weather guys, Stan must have thought to himself.

The fog cut New York City down to size. There was architectural equality in the gray mist that cut off the top of Manhattan's skyscrapers at the twentieth story. It also seemed to dampen the noise, like some cosmic blanket holding in the sound of horns and the grind of the eighteen wheelers.

I felt like the city. I felt the mist swirling around in my skull, distracting and hiding the truth. If Tommy didn't kill Pinto, then who did? If the mysterious Union for the Liberation of the Working Class killed Pinto, why hadn't they come forward earlier? Was Noolan part of that group? Who firebombed my car, and why? Why would the ULWC want to kill

Wackley? Where the hell were they holding Tanya? What was I going to have for dinner?

I solved the last one by ducking into a deli on Twenty-third and ordering a lean pastrami on rye.

You want to be a policeman? I recognized the waiter as a guy I had once locked up for sawing off the heads of parking meters and busting them open in his house like his own personal piggy banks. In theory, I admired and supported his actions, if not his motives. It was lunacy to shell out tax money for highways, registration, licenses, to pay gasoline sales taxes and still have to cough up quarters for the privilege of parking my car on a city street. So go ahead and slash off the heads of those one-nosed bandits—but you can't do it on my beat.

Now here we were, a decade or so later, and the guy is going to be serving my food. I put this guy away for two and a half years and now he's the man who will be handling the food that will go into my stomach.

The kicker was that because I was a single, I got a table right away. I glided past the line up near the register of ten or so other deli afficionados, who stared at me with resigned envy as I was ushered to my table. I could have walked out, but my stomach said stick around.

I buried my face in the menu and gave him the order. He was a medium-built Rican who gave no indication that he knew me. I was feeling better about my decision.

Whoever had had the seat before me left a newspaper; I picked it up and glanced at it. The number-one story was about the rally for America. Tomorrow was the big day, and they already had an advance sale that would fill the Garden to capacity. A list of acts appeared in the story, and I wasn't surprised to see that most of the names were completely new to me. I started to feel very old.

The vice president's name I did know. He would be at the rally to give the keynote address. The president was off in Vienna, but he'd be speaking via satellite hookup.

Sprinkled throughout the story were references to the late Ned Pinto and how dear to his heart was this call to patriotism. Bert Sloan was mentioned as head of the Make America Better Committee, along with the late superstar's wife, Tanya.

I got my pastrami a little fattier than I liked it, but the beer was cold and made it go down easier. When the waiter handed me the check, we exchanged some small talk about the weather. "You look like someone . . ." he said, "but I can't quite place you."

I shrugged and found my way back to my car. The short run to the office took an extra ten minutes because people were having trouble making out the stoplights in the mist.

I played back my phone messages and the mystery of Carol Simmons was solved. She let me know that she was in Jersey talking to her mother. She hoped to be able to give me a little green sometime tomorrow. Then there were two hang-ups, and a pitch by a life insurance salesman, who asked that I call him back for an *extraordinary* deal.

The phone rang the second I turned the answering machine off. It was Sloan, who admitted calling a couple of times during the afternoon. That accounted for the hang-ups.

"I didn't call you on the pager because I haven't heard from the ULWC. You've been gone a long time. Did you pick up anything?" He sounded desperate.

I could have asked him how I could have picked up anything. All I had to go on was a tape showing a small room, a desk, a Bulova clock, and Tanya tied to a wooden chair. Did he expect me to start canvassing all the hotel rooms in the tri-state area? Instead I reported that I was in a holding pattern for the time being.

"Anything come through on the videotape?"

"It's being processed. I don't expect any news for at least four more hours."

"Oh, I see." He sounded disappointed. "Please call me as soon as you know something."

I told him I would.

I called Gellet's studio, and the Frenchman came on. "Zlots, what ees wrong with zose crazy people?" He had been monitoring the ULWC propaganda line. "Tze United States ees a great country. Ze fools should live een in a place where tzere ees tze communism. Zen tzey would see!"

"I agree with you, Alain. How's it going?"

"Slowly, but steadily. Zere are some interesting tzings zat may be of some help. You will decide what ees a clue and what ees not."

"Give me an idea."

"Zere is a zound which reoccurs every forty seconds or so. I tzink it ees tze zound of an airplane."

"That would mean something in the flight pattern of Kennedy or LaGuardia. Newark doesn't have that many flights coming in and out. What else?"

"Zere ees a lot of very deep bass zounds, which would suggest zat tze room ees near a highway zat sees lots of truck traffic."

"Okay, Alain. You're narrowing it down."

"You know Zlots, I am working now only on tze low end of ze scale. I have to work my way to ze higher pitches."

"Just do what you have to. When do you think you might be finished?"

"Hmm, let's zee. Eet is a quarter to zeven . . . Would you want to come tomorrow in ze A.M. or do you want to come here zis evening? I will be working all night."

"I'd rather make it this evening," I told him.

"Yes, yes, of course. Ze lady's life ees in danger. Come tzen at two," he told me.

I batted the facts of the case around for another few minutes. Then I locked the front door and pulled out the convertible couch for a catnap.

The fog had been blown away for the most part when I reached All Alain's Art Studio on Fourteenth. There was a residue of moisture on the streets and on the cars, making sparkling reflections in the light of the streetlamps.

Alain was waiting for me and had set up a digital compact disk player. In addition, the Frenchman had just brewed a pot of steaming coffee.

He handed me a cup, making a face. "I do not know if what I have for you will be helpful." He shrugged. "I could not find anything which would make ze location easier."

"I used up my quota of miracles on the Mets during the playoffs and the series last year," I said with a half smile.

"Ah, listen to zis."

He pressed a button and I heard a clicking sound. Alain amplified it and then slowed it down so it was possible to hear each individual click.

"What the hell is that?"

"You know Zlots, zese video cameras have omnidirection microphones. Tzerefore, I would zay that zis noise came from ze person holding ze camera, because eet was close to ze mike."

"Yeah, but what is it?"

"Eet is ze zound of metal clicking together, small pieces, like coins. But it ees close to ze mike, like I said, zo I don't tzink it ees coins. *Non*, I tzink it ees jewelry, perhaps a necklace or a bracelet zat moves when ze camera ees moved."

"That might mean the person holding the camera is a woman."

Alain shrugged. "Here ees sometzing else from ze person holding ze camera."

The four large speakers blasted out the sound of a watch ticking.

"Eet is a watch, of course, but zere is something I can tell by zis kind of ticking. The cameraperson ees wearing ze watch, and ze watch ees a spring mechanism, which must be wound. Eet is not a battery-run quartz."

I nodded. "Anything else?"

"Here you have a zound. Eet is like a cough, *non?* Now we use a filter and try it like zis."

It was the unmistakable sound of an auto ignition.

"Zis hapened two more times during zis tape. Zis room ees near a garage or a parking lot, close to the ground floor."

I had a good picture now. "Everything points to a motel. There are a lot of them on the Kennedy-LaGuardia flight path. There are main truck routes right along that path, too."

"Zat would make sense," Gellet agreed.

I took a sip of the coffee Alain had brewed; it was strong and hot. It was times like this that you wanted the resources of the FBI. With their money and manpower, they would assign a man to every motel. One- or two-hundred-man details were no problem to them.

"Ze man used helium to alter his voice. I have tried to make an approximation of what ze voice would zound like wizzhout ze gas."

I heard the diatribe again, but this time it came in a deep monotone.

"Zis is mostly guesswork Zlots, so I cannot zay how close eet would be to ze actual voice," Gellet apologized.

"I can't recognize it," I told him.

He flicked another switch. "All right, zere is one

more zing zat might help. Here ees anozzer zound zat lasted for three seconds."

I listened to a high-pitched chirping. It was a sound which was familiar, but it threw me for the moment. "I've heard it before, but I can't place it," I said.

Gellet touched his wrist. "Eet is a wristwatch alarm. Zis watch is farther from ze camera: perhaps eet is ze man who is speaking?"

I remembered the Bulova said five thirty, and that was the time her daily alarm went off for her vitamins. "No, that would be Tanya's."

"Well zen Zlots, my apologies for not being able to geeve you more information."

"You've been very helpful, Alain. I've got the pieces, and now it's just a matter of putting them together."

Just then I heard another sound similar to the watch alarm. "That sounds like a different kind of alarm. Can you amplify it?" I asked him.

"I'm afraid not, my friend." Alain laughed. "Zat is ze pager you are wearing on your belt."

I joined him in the laugh and then went to the phone in his outer office. Sloan picked it up on the first ring.

"I'm damn glad to hear from you. They called me, the ULWC. They've given up on the idea to cancel the rally. Now they want money in exchange for Tanya."

"I thought they would. How much?"

"A million! In fifty- and one-hundred-dollar denominations."

"And they want it by when?"

"Ten this morning."

· ·

19

Sloan led me into the suite and asked if I wanted a drink. The guy seemed on the verge of a breakdown. His hands shook as he poured out his Scotch and he absentmindedly asked again if I wanted an eye-opener. I refused him the second time too.

The seven-hundred-buck-a-night room stank from cigarettes and stale booze. I waited for him to guzzle down his nerve tonic, which he did in two long gulps. He yawned, rubbed his eyes with the back of his hands, and looked up at me. "It's been a nightmare," he said. There were dark circles around his eyes, and bags that Colonel Tetley could have used for his tea.

I settled on the sofa and nodded in agreement. "Let's hear the tape, Bert," I said softly.

He brought the recorder I had given him over to the coffee table. "The bastards want a million bucks," he said, as if he couldn't believe it.

"They don't get anything until we know Tanya's alive," I told him. I pressed Play and old Helium

Voice got on. I reminded myself that I would never watch a Donald Duck cartoon again.

The tape was standard operating procedure as far as kidnappings go. First came the justification, which was that Tanya represented a warmongering class elite intent on destroying the workers. Then came the threat that she would be dismembered alive and a piece of her body would be delivered every day. As the ads for the horror flicks say, not for the squeamish. There was a pause of a few seconds while Tanya's abductor got a second wind. In this case it was helium wind.

The meat of the demands followed: he, or they, wanted a million bucks in untraceable cash, fifties and hundreds, delivered by ten A.M. to a location of their choosing. A single unarmed courier was to make the drop. The girl would be released uninjured if they got the money. There was the usual rider that if the police were notified, Tanya would be killed immediately, and very unpleasantly. The last line on the tape was a warning to stand by the phone for further instructions.

"What do you think?" Sloan asked me.

"I think we'd better come up with a million bucks."

He nodded. "It's not going to be easy. There's money in the Command Studio accounts, but that means signing papers, getting board approval, converting stocks into cash. . . . Of course, I'll have to say why it's needed, and then the whole damn thing will leak." He fumbled for a cigarette and lit it, using both hands to steady the match. "Then again, we could . . ." He floated off like the smoke, deep in thought.

"Could what?" I prodded loudly.

He seemed to snap back. "Well, we could borrow a million based on the gate receipts and the TV rights."

I wondered how Tanya would feel about her release buying guns and bombs and whatever else a terrorist organization needed to finance their work, but I let it pass.

Sloan was thinking out loud. "I can't possibly get all that together by ten, though, and the rally starts at one."

"I'll make it for twelve. They have to give us proof that Tanya's alive, and she has to be released before they get the money."

"Will they go for it?"

"They have to: we've got them over a barrel."

"Come again," Sloan said.

"Look, their first ploy was to stop the rally, but now that that's failed, they want money to save face. Killing her wouldn't accomplish anything; they could have killed her the first minute they had a chance to. No, they want the money, and we'll oblige them if they meet our conditions."

"We can't play around with Tanya's life! No amount of money in the world is worth Tanya's life," Sloan insisted nervously.

"Sloan, we do this my way or you find someone else. My way says that Tanya is already dead; if they show me that she's not, then they have to prove to me that she won't be as soon as we turn over the money. We're not forking over a million for a corpse. As long as they know their demands will be met, there's an incentive not to kill her."

He looked at me as if he wanted to say something, but he thought better of it. He took a deep drag on his cigarette and jabbed it out in the ashtray. The guy's nerves seemed ready to snap.

"If you've got another line in the bedroom, why don't you wake some people up and try to make arrangements for the money," I told him.

"Yeah, okay."

He stood up, poured what was left in the bottle into his glass, and retreated into the bedroom.

I played the tape back four times and tried to pick

up anything that might give me insight as to where the call was being made. If there was anything there, it needed Alain's sophisticated ear to be discovered. In the other room, I could hear Sloan making the arrangements for the money. I settled back on the plush sofa and waited. My watch read four fifteen. That left less than six hours, by the kidnappers' original instructions.

My thoughts drifted back to Tanya and her visit to my office. She had tried to get me to take her case and protect her from precisely what had happened to her. Had I kept the money and told her I would do it, her being kidnapped would have been my responsibility. Of course, I wouldn't have let her go jogging around Central Park, even with O'Keefe as an escort. That bothered me.

Tanya was obviously the kind of person who took care of herself. She exercised, took her daily dose of megavitamins, and was concerned enough about the death threat to seek me out. Why then make herself such an easy target in the park?

Of course, I had to remember where Tanya was from. The cold, gray Moscow weather wasn't conducive to outdoor exercise, except maybe ice hockey and other winter sports. The confining surroundings of the Soviet Union were a far cry from the wide-open sunny clime of California. Tanya might have felt the need to just get out and run. And she must have felt safe with ex-marine Dennis O'Keefe.

I looked at the phone and ordered it to ring. It just stared back at me.

I thought about putting a trace on the line and decided it didn't pay. There wasn't a person in the country who didn't know that phone lines could be traced. It took significantly longer than was shown in the movies and on TV, and if the trace did work, most of the time it was off by a digit or two. Invariably you ended up busting into the home of a little old lady who took care of stray cats and whose husband was a deacon.

Even so, any hood knows you use a pay phone if you're calling with some nefarious scheme. It had become part of the gene pool of the American hoodlum, wrapped up tightly in the DNA. If you present ransom demands, use a pay phone! It's probably taught in Kidnapping 101.

I was going nuts staring at the phone. Come on and ring, damn you! I decided that if I ever caught these bastards, I'd have the judge tack on another six months to their sentence and tell them there was the possibility of a pardon, but only if they'd sit by the phone and wait for the governor's call.

Another half hour went by, and I found myself dozing. I walked into the bathroom, and as I splashed some cold water on my face, I caught my reflection in the glass. I looked like hell. The cool blues were riddled with bloodshot lines. The black hair with the distinguished gray touches was messy, sporting a cowlick in the back. The puss showed a day-and-a-half growth of beard. I looked like Sal "the Barber" Maglie, the New York Giants pitcher who wouldn't shave for three days before he pitched so he would look mean to the opposing hitters. They called him the Barber because if you dug yourself into the batter's box, he'd brush you back and give you a fastball shave.

I went back to my post and stared again at the dark brown hotel phone that had become my nemesis. Time for a new tactic, Slots old boy. Time for the power of positive thinking.

The phone will ring . . . the phone will ring . . . ring phone . . . Now!

Whattaya know. It did.

Sloan came running out of the bedroom like a wild man. He looked at the phone, then at me. "Pick it up, damm it!" he yelled.

I held up my hand. "Take it easy, take it easy. We don't want to appear too anxious."

I let it ring twice more. Sloan looked like he was going to have a stroke. "Yeah," I said into the mouthpiece.

"Sloan?" It was Donald Duck again.

"I'm taking the call," I said.

"Who are you?"

"Resnick. I'm a friend of Tanya's and Sloan's. I'm not a cop, so don't get spooked."

"I deal only with Sloan."

"Then you don't deal at all, friend."

I hung up.

Sloan's eyes bugged out of his head. "Are you crazy?" he sputtered. I didn't answer.

The phone rang again almost immediately.

"You do that again, Resnick, and the lady gets cut up into little slivers and fed to the fish!" Donald was angry.

"You've got my attention, and I'm getting your money. You don't get fifties, because it makes it too heavy for one man to carry. You get a million in hundreds, unmarked, not traceable. And you deal with me from now on. If the girl is okay, you get your money. If the goods are damaged, you get shit."

There was a long pause.

"We'll deal with you, Resnick, and the girl is okay."

"I want to hear her on the phone."

"That can be arranged."

"It's got to be in person, or a tape of her reading this morning's headlines from the *Times*. You fellows ever hear of the *Times?* It's a newspaper; you can buy it in the same store you get your comic books."

"What else do you want, Mr. Wiseass?"

"Ten o'clock is too early. We've got to swing a deal with the banks and that means twelve at the earliest."

"I don't like your attitude."

"You're breaking my heart."

"I think I'm going to hang up and start slicing Golden Girl up for fish bait."

"Sure you are. You're going to blow your chance to squeeze a million bucks out of the capitalist warmongers because you don't like my fresh-mouth attitude. A million bucks buys a lot of hammers and sickles, not to mention M-16s. You call us back at eight and I want to hear Tanya alive and well. Otherwise, we go straight to the feds."

I hung up.

Sloan was looking green around the gills.

"It'll be okay," I assured him. "Just come up with the money, or these fellows are going to be a trifle peeved."

There were two phone calls that came in around eight: one was from Sloan's sound man at the Garden, who complained about the cooperation he was getting from his crew; the other was a genuine wrong number.

As eight rolled into eight-thirty, Sloan responded by chain-smoking and flashing me dirty looks. By nine o'clock some of my confidence had drained off and the first seeds of doubt started to buzz around in my brain.

Then the call came.

There was no hello, and thankfully my helium friend wasn't on the line. It was a tape recording of Tanya. Her voice sounded strong, although she seemed a little bit tired.

"Consumer Price Index rises three tenths of one percent for third gain in three months," she read dully.

I looked over at the *Times* that room service had sent up. The headline was there.

"I'm feeling well and I'm being treated well. You are to go to your office Mr. Resnick, and get a message there. You will be followed every step of the way." She sounded as if she were reading from a set of instructions. "If anyone follows you, I will be killed immediately. Just before you are to deliver the money, I will be released. There will be instructions for you to confirm the release."

The line went dead.

I played the tape back for Sloan.

"Thank God she seems all right." He appeared to be back in control again. "The money should be here in the next fifteen minutes," he said, checking his watch.

"Fine. We'll put it in some very beat-up piece of luggage. The last thing in the world we want to do is have some mugger come along and try to rob me."

Sloan stared at me in that funny way people have when they want to say something but they're not sure how you'll take it.

"You've got something on your mind, Bert. You might as well spill it."

"Well, I was just thinking about that other case you had some years back when you recovered fifty million bucks. . . ."

"Yeah, we got every cent of it back."

"Remember I asked you if you were tempted to just take the money and disappear? This gives you a second chance, doesn't it? I mean, if you ever had any regrets about your decision . . ."

"Come on, Bert. Why the hell would I want to go to Tahiti and spend the rest of my life on sun-drenched beaches living like a king when I have the chance to be tortured or killed by a group of left-wing fanatics right here?"

"You're kidding, right?"

"Sure. Too much sun is bad for the skin."

20

. . . .

The million bucks was crammed into two medium-size Samsonites. I counted the money myself and had Sloan recount it. Then I bucked the crosstown traffic to my office.

It made good sense on their part to send me back to my office for the next message. They would have my block staked out and know if anyone who looked suspicious was around. I figured they would get my address from the book or from Tanya, and then let me know where the drop was to take place. If they were watching my office, there would be no tap on the line, and the only one who would know the destination of the drop would be me. I was sure that I would be followed right up to the destination. There would probably be a telescopic sight aimed at me, the cross hairs making a part in my scalp.

The little light on my answering machine was blinking up a storm. I hit Replay and listened to the first message, which was from Sherry, wanting to know where the hell I was at seven in the morning.

The underlying tone was *Who the hell are you out sleeping with?*

Call number two was from Carol Simmons, who wanted me to know that she had a little surprise for me.

Call number three came from the kidnappers. It was a short message, brief and to the point: "Fifty-six Water Street. If you're there after twelve thirty, don't bother. There's a pay phone on the northeast corner. Look under the phone."

I had over an hour to kill. I called Sherry at her office and told her what had happened. I could tell she didn't like the idea of me going it alone. "Why don't you call the FBI to give you backup, just in case? They deal with this kind of thing all the time."

That was all I needed: twenty-four guys in beige Palm Beach suits with mirrored sunglasses, black shoes, and walkie-talkies in their right butt pockets. There was the old story about a federal agent who went down to the local precinct and dressed down the men at roll call. The Bureau was in the middle of a very important surveillance job and he didn't want any of the local men to stumble into their area and throw a fright into the suspect. "This fellow is expected to be in Times Square at noon, so I'm going to warn all of you to stay out of Times Square," he bellowed. Afterward, he walked over to the captain. "By the way, Captain, just where the hell is this Times Square?"

"I can handle it alone," I told Sherry. "If it screws up, I've got only myself to blame."

I made a date with Sherry that evening and she blew me a kiss over the phone for luck. "You call me the very second it's all over," she said. "Do you understand that, Slots Resnick? The *very second!*"

I promised and hung up.

I tried Simmons again, but no one answered. I would have liked to have given her the good news about her brother. His legal woes weren't over, but he sure looked a lot better on the murder rap. I thought about the surprise she had for me. Maybe her mother had loosened the purse strings after all.

Water Street was a rolling block with dingy gray fronts and black-painted windows. The air smelled of salt water, fish, and the nearby rotting planks of the docks. Not too far away a tugboat chugged along and a deep basso foghorn bleated every fifteen seconds, even though the air was crystal clear. Fifty-six Water was located next to a seamen's diner. There was a junk-strewn vacant lot between the diner and a soup kitchen on the other side.

I walked up to the two doors under the number. One led to a ground-floor office and the other, a solid metal garage-type door, fronted the warehouse. A two-by-four with the company's name, WONG & NG IMPORT-EXPORT, written in thick black crayon hung over the doors.

I was tempted to walk in, but the instructions said to find the phone on the northeast corner. I walked over to the phone and looked under the coin box. There was a note pasted to the underbelly. CALL SLOAN, it ordered.

I patted myself down for quarters and came up with three dimes instead. That took me to Information—I'd forgotten to take Sloan's number with me—and the Hyatt's front desk. They patched me through, and Sloan picked up after the first ring.

"What happened?" I asked him.

"She's free! She just called me from Asbury Park. They released her unharmed, thank God. She says she wants to come to the Garden. She's going to flag down a cab and shoot right down here. It wasn't a setup. She was calling from a diner, and I could hear lots of people in the background." There was a mixture of relief and joy in his voice.

"Okay, that's what I wanted to know."

"Slots, she said you'd be calling. They gave her a message for you, which she made me write down. Hold on a minute." Sloan's voice grew somber. "Okay, she said to tell you that they've been following you since you left the hotel. To prove it, they say you're wearing a brown jacket over cocoa slacks. You're to walk over to the address they gave you and open the door—the warehouse door, and walk in. You are not to let go of the bags until you're told to. If you make a move to leave the area, or reach for a gun, there's a man with a rifle who will blow your head off."

"That's not very friendly."

"Slots, be careful . . . and thanks," Sloan said sincerely.

"Yeah, see you soon."

I placed the receiver back in its cradle and headed back toward Wong & Ng.

The street was empty even though it was midday. I gripped the two pieces of Samsonite, and feeling like Willie Loman doing *High Noon*, I made my way to the door. Somewhere above or around me, a man was perched cradling a rifle.

Naturally, it was at that moment that I had to scratch my nose in the worst way. If I put down the bag, would my rifle-toting shadow give me a chance to rub the old proboscus, or would he take the lowering of the suitcase as a signal to start the hunting season? I decided that an infuriating itch beat a ventilated skull.

The door itself was open about two inches. I held on to my luggage and pushed it open with the toe of my shoe. It seemed pitch black inside, and then something darted out toward me.

Blinding light exploded from a spot not more than three feet in front of my eyes. I jumped back reflexively, but a strong hand grabbed me by the throat and threw me forward. The door slammed behind me. My senses had the few seconds necessary to figure out what happened: they had shot off a flashbulb as I entered the warehouse. It had left me totally blind.

The two satchels were taken out of my hands, and to be sure I wouldn't be neglected, I felt the cold steel of a gun barrel placed at a spot between my throat and my chin. I was patted down professionally and the reassuring weight of the detective's special was removed from my shoulder holster. I had no idea if there were one, two, or three people in the room with me. The bright yellow ball hanging in front of my eyes was slowly changing to orange and red.

Pow! Another flash went off and it set back my recovery period.

This time keep your eyes closed, Resnick, I told myself.

I was pushed against what felt like a large burlap beanbag. I fell down hard and my body made an indentation: coffee beans.

This time I kept my eyes closed and watched the pretty colored suns go from white to yellow to orange to red. I opened one eye, fully expecting the flash again but it didn't happen. I tentatively opened the other eye. I started to make out objects.

I was in a big dank room filled with jars of food, novelty items, and small furniture. Some of the stuff seemed to be falling out of packing crates. I was lying against a very large burlap bag of coffee, one of three that I could see in the warehouse. To the right of the bags was a wall of cartons. The only pieces of usable furniture were a scarred rolltop desk and a broken wicker chair.

The two Samsonite cases were on the floor, opened. The million bucks was as out of place on the dirty warehouse floor as a fat man in a marathon race.

The gun was back, tucked under my chin like a bib. My eyes traveled from the hand holding it, up the forearm to the shoulder, from the shoulder to the neck, from there to the face of—Dennis O'Keefe.

"Keep still, pal. Try one of your cute tricks and I'll split you open like a watermelon. Sit forward and put both hands behind your back. That's a good boy. Now hold your wrists still."

I felt him cuff me. That wasn't too bright. You don't cuff a man's hands behind his back. It's too easy to bring them behind his legs and then he steps out of them. The proper way was to cuff the wrist to the ankle. My sense of hope was short-lived, however.

O'Keefe clamped another set of cuffs around my right ankle and shackled me to a three-inch water pipe that the bag was leaning on.

"I owe you one, don't I, Resnick!" he said menacingly.

He drew his hand back and then swung out with a roundhouse. He stopped it an inch from my jaw, laughing at the way I flinched.

"Scared, huh?" he said, thoroughly enjoying himself.

Sure I was scared: not of his mock punch, but because O'Keefe didn't even care to disguise himself. That was bad news for me. It meant that I wasn't going to get out of there alive to identify him.

Sloan hadn't been told where I was going, and although the message was on the answering machine in my office, my sensible habit of locking the door negated any chance of anyone's hearing it and tracking me down. No cavalry was going to come to the rescue, and I was trussed up like a Christmas turkey. The odds left something to be desired.

"So you're the United Liberators of the Working Class," I said, stalling.

"There's a hell of a lot of us, Resnick." O'Keefe went to the million and started counting. "If I'm short here, you're going to die slow," he said.

"Your organization killed Pinto?"

"*I* killed Pinto," he said coolly. "He had been sentenced to death by the tribunal, and I was chosen to be his executioner."

"What about Noolan?"

O'Keefe pulled out three packages, counting the ten thousand in each. Then he counted the number of ten-thousand-dollar packages and satisfied himself that it added up to a million. "Tommy was given two chances and he wasn't able to do the job. He was incompetent," he said when he'd finished.

"How come he never mentioned the ULWC?"

"Because it didn't serve our interests," O'Keefe snapped. "We wanted the world to think that Ned Pinto was killed by one of his own kind, a so-called war hero, who killed the patriots of the People's Republic of Vietnam. At least Noolan knew how to accept the role of Ned's killer."

"You were afraid of the backlash at the rally if Ned was gunned down by a left-winger. That's why you and Wackley warned me off the case. You thought I was getting too close to the truth."

"You're not stupid, Resnick. We had heard of your reputation."

"Then Wackley was in it with you. I thought the two of you were supposed to be Pinto's friends."

O'Keefe laughed. "We cultivated the friendship. We were told to gain Ned's confidence, and we did."

"Did you cultivate Wackley, too? He was your lover, wasn't he?"

O'Keefe's eyes narrowed. I expected him to run

over and pop me, but he didn't. Instead, he smiled and took a seat in the wicker chair.

"We were right about you: you do your homework. Yes, I was in love with William." His lips tightened in a grimace. "He was a great disappointment to the movement—and to me personally. He objected to placing a bomb in your car. When that Tucker was killed, he threatened that he would report the organization to the police. You see, he wanted out. He wanted out of the movement, and his relationship with me. Would you like to know why?"

"I seem to be at your disposal," I said.

"He began to consort with the enemy. He had planned to marry Arlene Diamond and become an exploiter like Sloan and Tanya."

"So you were appointed his executioner, too?"

"I was proud and pleased to do it," he responded.

"I guess you'll be proud and pleased to execute me as well."

He stared at me and shook his head. "You're not worth killing. You're going to be much more valuable to us. You see, there's been a change in our philosophy. The time is now right for the ULWC to publicize our efforts on behalf of the downtrodden. We hope that people will gain courage from our exploits and join us in the great battle to overthrow the capitalists and give power and wealth back to the masses."

"You're nuts."

"All revolutionaries from Lenin to Castro have been called names, Resnick. All you have to do is to make sure that everyone knows that the ULWC is responsible for whatever happens today."

"What the hell is that supposed to mean?"

"You'll find out. The world will soon find out."

O'Keefe closed the two Samsonite bags and carried them to the door.

"How do I spread the word about your wonderful

group if I'm handcuffed to a water pipe for the rest of my life?"

"Once we accomplish our task, the police will be called and told of your whereabouts," he said.

The door closed behind him and I was left in pitch darkness. It was a metal door and the warehouse was well insulated. I could yell my head off for all the good it would do.

I went over O'Keefe's story and tried to picture Dennis on the bike. He was bigger in the shoulders than Noolan, and although I could understand Boddiker making a mistake in identifying Noolan, why wouldn't Sloan see it was O'Keefe? O'Keefe could have been wearing a blond wig, and it did happen very fast. The idea of the wig brought me back to the fact that O'Keefe hadn't tried to disguise his identity at all.

I remembered the call I had made by hitting "redial" on the phone in his apartment. He wasn't concerned about being identified because he was going to be leaving the country, probably headed for the Virgin Islands. O'Keefe would probably carry out that big action he had been talking about, take a cut out of the million and head for the white beaches of Saint Thomas.

In the meantime, I was anchored to a water pipe and forced to wait for Denny's call to the cops to set me free.

I tried yanking the pipe but it wouldn't budge. I attempted to slip my hands out of the cuffs, but O'Keefe had made them too tight. I was about to give up when I heard the sound of glass breaking. It was fairly close by, on the other side of the cartons. I held my breath and listened carefully. It sounded like someone was talking. I called out for help.

Carol Simmons and Mildos strolled into the warehouse. Simmons and Mildos weren't exactly my idea of Batman and Robin, but they were certainly a dynamic duo just then.

"Slots, what the hell are you up to?" Carol asked me.

"You're not shot or anything, are you?" Mildos wanted to know. "I've been known to faint at the sight of blood."

"I'm just hog-tied, Don. Look the pipe over and see if there's any way to saw through it."

Carol checked the handcuffs on my wrist. "Where's the key?" she asked.

"He probably took it with him."

"Who?"

"This fellow, Dennis O'Keefe."

"There's no way you can break through this pipe," Mildos said, kneeling next to us.

"Well, how the hell do we get you loose, Slots? You sure he didn't throw the key somewhere?" Carol got up and started looking around on the floor. There was light coming from beyond the cartons, but most of the warehouse was still in the dark.

"How did you find me?" I asked them, "and how did you get in here?"

"We decided it would be fun to play detective," Don said coyly.

Carol sighed. "Mildos, why don't you give it a rest? It was like this, Slots: I was coming over to your place to give you something." She pulled a check out of her pocket. "I didn't feel right about you working and not getting paid. My mother came across with fifty bucks."

"You should be honored, Slots. This is the first time that I remember Carol's money not going straight up her nose."

"Look who's talking! I walked into his house and saw him snorting up the sugar bowl."

"I was drunk, you bitch!"

"Come on, children. I'm still waiting to find out how you stumbled upon me," I said.

"As I was saying before I was so rudely interrupted, I was going over to your office to hand you my mother's check. Donald offered to drive me, since I don't have a car anymore."

"Nor a license, I may add, but that never stopped you," Mildos piped in.

Carol looked exasperated but she continued. "Anyway, we were circling around the block looking for a place to park when I saw you walk out of your office with suitcases."

"Please, can I tell the rest? Can I?"

"You might as well. You'll just interrupt me anyhow."

"I said, 'Looky, Carol. It looks like Slots is going on vacation.' Carol said that didn't make any sense, since you were working on the case. I said maybe it had something to do with the case and suggested that we follow you."

"What he said was, 'Goody, Goody, let's have some fun and follow him,'" Carol explained disgustedly.

Mildos shrugged. "I love adventure," he said, rolling his eyes.

Carol went over to the rolltop desk and tentatively raised the accordian cover.

"You mean the two of you followed me down here?" That didn't fit. Where was the guy with the rifle? How come they released Tanya? I was sure that Carol and Don left a lot to be desired in the area of undercover surveillance.

"Look what I found!" Carol called out. She held up two boxes with pictures of handcuffs on them. O'Keefe had apparently bought the handcuffs and tossed the boxes into the desk. "And look what else I got!" She held up two small keys.

Mildos took one from her and tried to unlock the ankle cuffs. Carol took the other and fiddled with the lock on my wrists.

"This one doesn't want to open," Mildos said.

"Switch keys," I told them.

This time Carol got the cuffs on my wrists to spring open. Mildos followed suit. I stood up, bending to rub my ankles. The cuffs had been tighter than I thought. I found my gun in one of the small drawers in the desk.

"Okay, you followed me. Now, how did you get in here?"

"Come here and I'll show you," Carol said.

I went with her past the cartons. There was a connecting door between the warehouse and the adjacent office. Mildos had broken a pane of glass on the door, opened it, and they'd walked into the office and through the connecting door to the warehouse. "We were looking for you, and then I heard you yell," Carol told me.

We stepped out of the Wong & NG emporium and onto Water Street.

I broke the good news to Carol about her brother and received a tearful buss on the cheek and a warm thank you. I also told her that Dennis O'Keefe admitted to killing Ned. I advised her to call Bunny Fleischer and let her know about it.

Mildos asked me if I wanted a lift. He pointed to a '56 Chevy, pink and white, in immaculate condition.

"That's a beauty," I said, genuinely impressed.

"I'm a connoisseur of fine things," he replied in that pompous way of his.

"It's his father's car, and he's away for the week," Carol told me.

That clinched it for me. The so-called ULWC had to be very sure of itself. They had to know that I wasn't going to call the police, and they had to know that I was bringing the money. They had made a point of describing what I was wearing, so one of them must have seen me.

If I was being tailed by them, how could they miss Mildos's car? It stood out like a nun at an orgy. If I wasn't being tailed, how did they know they could release Tanya?

I was starting to get the idea that the ULWC was composed of O'Keefe and whoever it was that was holding the camera that made the videotape Alain and I had listened to.

"I know I can't repay you for what you did for Tommy and me," Carol said, "but at least this is a start." She handed the check to me.

"Tommy still has a gun charge to contend with, even if he's off the hook with the murder. Carol, did he ever talk to you about a left-leaning organization called the Union for the Liberation of the Working Class?"

"What? Are you nuts! Tommy didn't know a thing about politics. He'd been a loner all his life until he got hung up on being the savior of the Vietnam vets. All he ever wanted was to be left alone. Sure, his Vietnam experience scrambled his thoughts now and again, but you could never even get him in a room with more than two people. Even this Vietnam thing was something he was doing alone, to satisfy his own feelings of injustice. Tommy could never be a joiner. Trust me on this, there's more chance of Mildos turning straight than Tommy belonging to a Red conspiracy."

Mildos pouted. "Heaven forbid! Bite your tongue!"

"Yeah, that's what I thought."

I pocketed the check, more to safeguard Carol from buying coke than for my own financial gain.

The next logical person to interview would be Tanya Pinto, and Sloan had said she was going to be at the rally. "I'll take my own car up to the Garden,"

I said. "I'm glad the two of you came along when you did."

I didn't burst their bubble by telling them that their stumbling in on a ransom payment could have caused the deaths of both me and Tanya. All's well that ends well, they say.

"If you ever need a partner . . ." was Mildos's parting shot as he walked toward his father's car.

"Don't push your luck, Don!" Carol said, reading my mind.

21

• •

I drove north on the FDR and made it as far as Fourteenth Street, where all traffic came to a dead stop. I could look up the incline about a mile ahead and it was like a still life, *Traffic Going North*.

I glanced down at the steering wheel and noted the red welt on my wrist from the handcuffs. The fact that Simmons and Mildos came along and got me out of the cuffs didn't mean much. At best, it bought me a few hours before O'Keefe and whoever else it was that made up the ULWC pulled off their great coup.

I was to be the mouthpiece, O'Keefe had said, the chronicler who would tell the story of how the ULWC masterminded . . . what?

I closed my eyes and thought about it. A cacaphony of auto horns blared around me. This wasn't any accident-caused jam: this one was a planned, predetermined, screwup. If a car breaks down, or the highway gets a two-inch puddle, a couple of lanes back up, maybe even all three for a few minutes. But most of the time you're in a slow-moving queue in which it becomes mandatory to gawk at the fender bender or cuss out some poor slob who forgot to put enough gas in his tank. This one though was something special. There wasn't the slightest bit of movement, and from the looks of things, that's how it was going to be for a long while.

I turned the knob on the radio, hoping for a traffic report. I never had luck with those things. They either gave the traffic on the other side of town or told me too late what streets to avoid as I sat stuck in an island of cars.

I played spin the knob until I hit a station that promised a helicopter traffic bulletin after this. "This" turned out to be a public service announcement on AIDS, a plug for the station's morning guy, and commercials for Burger King, a soft drink, and an outfit that promised financial security if you bought municipal bonds. Then came a half minute of weather, and finally they switched to Bill something-or-other in the chopper.

"Stay off the drive! That's my advice to all motorists this afternoon. We've got the vice president coming in for the big rally at the Garden and the FDR is backed up from the Sixties to the Twenties."

I knew that politicians who came up from Washington took the shuttle to LaGuardia and then were ferried over from the Queens airport by helicopter, which landed at the Thirty-fourth Street heliport. It was standard procedure for the police department to close the drive until the dignitary and his motorcade passed through. At least Sloan and Tanya would be happy that they were able to carry on the rally without a hitch.

It came to me with the force of thunder and lightning and the sound of clashing cymbals: *O'Keefe and the ULWC intended to kill the vice president.*

202

I snapped to attention. It made sense on all levels: O'Keefe promised a big media event that would shake the world; the ULWC had decided on going public to try to encourage all the fellow travelers who were keeping a low profile; the assassination of the vice president would certainly put the ULWC on the map.

This was the reason, then, that I wasn't killed! This wasn't to be a Lee Harvey Oswald kind of thing, where till this day his motives and political allegiance were a mystery. I was to be Boswell to O'Keefe's Samuel Johnson: it was going to be my job to tell all I knew about Denny and his organization.

He said the police would be around to release me later. Sure. *Later* meant after the assassination.

I was in the far outside lane and I knew that with the backup, it would take a good half hour just to get to the exit on Thirty-fourth Street. Then I'd have to make the crosstown trip to Eighth Avenue. There was no way I was going to get to the Garden before an hour, and an hour might be too late.

I was lucky enough to be in the outside lane, and better than that, there actually was a small shoulder that I could pull the car onto. My first instinct was to raise the hood, but I changed my mind, knowing that might be a signal to the auto strippers to ply their trade. Those guys were like buzzards, reducing a car to bare metal in a matter of minutes.

I parked and got out of the car, walking back past the stopped northbound cars, and dodging the speeding vehicles in the southbound lane. I walked past the projects and found myself on Sixteenth Street. It took another ten minutes to hail a cab, and the driver pocketed the ten I handed him to get me to the Felt Forum as fast as possible. Denny O'Keefe had scared me, but not as much as this guy. I was tempted to give him another ten to insure that I got to the Garden in one piece.

The marquee read RALLY FOR AMERICA, and there were two large American flags in front of the entrance. I jumped out of the cab and dashed into the lobby. A guard approached as I was explaining to the ticket taker that I was a guest of Mr. Sloan and Tanya Pinto.

"You gotta have a guest pass, Mac," he told me.

I walked him over to the side. "Why don't you pick up a house phone and talk to Bert Sloan?" I asked him. "I left the house in a hurry this morning and forgot my pass."

"Mr. Sloan is attending a reception right now. I couldn't get through to him if I wanted to."

"Where's the reception?"

"Third floor, VIP Lounge, but I can't let you up."

I thought of Herman Kelly. Kelly had worked in the police department for twelve years and then became one of the top men in the Madison Square Garden security operation. When I left the force, it was Herm who called me and wanted to know if I was interested in joining him at the Garden. "Why the hell not, Chief? I'll introduce you to Larry Bird when the Celtics come in here," Herm had offered.

But that was then, and this was now, and the *now* was running out of time.

"Look pal, I know you're doing your job, and I can respect that, but I've got to go up and see Sloan. Call Herm Kelly and ask him about me. Just do it, quick! Someone's life might be in danger."

"Sorry, you're out of luck. Herm Kelly retired three weeks ago. I gotta ask you to leave."

I handed him my private investigator card. "I'm in business now for myself. I used to be chief of detectives."

He shrugged. "Sorry pal, it don't ring a bell. I got guys with all kinds of things printed on cards to get them in to sold-out events. I stopped a guy last week dressed as a telephone repairman. He had on the uniform, the whole bit, with a phone sticking out of his back pocket. Another time a guy tries to make it through with a stethoscope around his neck. He says he's a heart specialist called in on an emergency."

The guard was leaving me no choice but to either deck him and make a dash for the door or pull out my gun and have him walk me through. Either way I was going to cause a ruckus and I'd be stopped before I made it upstairs.

He was staring at my card. "Resnick . . . Resnick . . . You related to a little shortstop used to play minor league ball? The guy had this funny handle. What the hell was it?"

"Slots?"

"Yeah, Slots!"

"That was me—I mean, that *is* me."

He looked me over. "Get out of here! But, damn, you could be him."

"I am him. I played short and second for the Gamers."

"I can't believe it! I was stationed down south in the service. I was a crazy baseball fan and I followed the kids in the minors. I figured I was like a scout spotting the future stars of the majors. What club did you wind up with?"

"I got cut down on a close play at second and tore up my leg. That was my career."

The guard shook his head. "Damn! That's too bad. I had you pegged with three stars. That's how I'd rate the prospects. I only rated one guy higher than you with three and a half stars, and that guy turned out to be Reggie Jackson."

"I'm flattered, uh . . ."

"Jack. Jack Reilly."

"Jack, I never thought anyone would remember me from those days. Look, I really have to see Sloan. What do you say?"

"Hell, get going! Sorry I gave you so much static. Good seeing you again, Slots."

I hustled inside and climbed the stairs two at a time to the third floor. The VIP Lounge was a beautifully appointed room where the Garden biggies would hold court with execs from Gulf & Western, the parent company. A sign on the door said COMMAND STUDIOS RECEPTION. There was a buffet table along one wall, and the well-dressed crowd was being served by red-jacketed waiters. I could see all this in quick glimpses, as the door was repeatedly being opened and closed by two beefy private guards, making sure they saw an invitation before they would let anyone in.

"The vice president come in yet?" You didn't have to be a rocket scientist to figure that Sloan and Tanya would fete the veep.

"Excuse me, sir. Do you have an invitation?" Tweedledum wanted to know.

"I'm a friend of Bert Sloan's."

"Sir, I wouldn't let God in here if he didn't have an invitation," Tweedledee said.

"Would you just take a look inside and ask Mr. Sloan to come out."

"Sorry, sir. I can't do that. Mr. Sloan isn't inside."

"How about Mrs. Pinto?"

"Sir, they're both at the press conference."

"Where's that?"

"One flight down in the Burgundy Room."

My first instinct was to run back down the stairs. The vice president would be meeting with the press and answering questions. But security there would be extremely tight. The only people allowed in that room, other than Tanya and Sloan, would be members of the working press. It made no sense for Denny to try anything in the airtight Burgundy Room, not when he would soon be rubbing elbows with the man at the reception being given by the

Command Studio brass. If there was going to be any action from O'Keefe, it would come at the reception.

I was about to delve into my bag of tricks to come up with a way to sashay past the guards when Arlene Diamond walked out. She was wearing a clinging black dress and carrying a black clutch purse.

"Ms. Diamond, do you remember me?"

She was already three sheets to the wind, but she staggered closer and looked me up and down. "Why, Mr. Resnick. So nice to see you."

"This gentleman wants to come to the reception, Ms. Diamond, but he doesn't have an invitation," Tweedledum explained.

"Oh, he's all right. I'll give him—(hic)—my invitation."

"Thanks," I told her.

The guards parted like the Red Sea and I stepped past them into the lounge with Arlene Diamond latched on to my elbow.

Once inside she patted my head. "Now have a good time, dear boy," she said as she turned and walked out again. I was convinced that although she knew my name, she hadn't the faintest idea who I was.

I went to the rear wall and leaned against it. I scanned the faces in the room but couldn't come up with Denny O'Keefe. I watched the bar, then I surveyed the little tables that were scattered all over the room. No O'Keefe.

There were about three hundred people in the room, so I started all over again, and got the same result. The Command Studio crowd headed for the bar, grabbed drinks, went over to the buffet table and had the waiters fill plates for them; then they grabbed tables and ate. Once they finished, they would rise and start the cycle all over again.

Icy fingers of doubt started playing the piano on

my spine. What if I was wrong about O'Keefe's target? What if O'Keefe had something totally different planned, and I was giving him valuable time to get away with it by not calling the police and warning them?

Then again, what could I say? If I told the cops that O'Keefe and the ULWC planned something big in the next couple of hours, what good would that do? What if I was wrong and O'Keefe *was* in on the press conference?

It was at that moment that I saw Denny—and he saw me. The reason I had missed him before was that I was looking for him among the guests. He had gotten a gold busboy's jacket and was mingling with the crowd, picking up dishes from the tables.

I saw him curse under his breath and move quickly in the direction of a side door. I toyed with the idea of pulling my piece, but there would be panic, and I wouldn't have been able to get off a clear shot. I followed him through the door and into a kitchen area.

It was here that the food for the reception was being prepared and the hors d'oeuvres heated for the trays. O'Keefe ran through the kitchen and out another door at the far end. As he ran, he tossed down what food he could from the tables, and I found myself slipping and sliding on a gooey mass of whipped cream cake and other assorted delicacies. A fellow in a white uniform and a chef's hat cursed me as I went flying by.

The far door led out to the corridor again. The building is circular, and O'Keefe maintained his distance. I kept catching the back of his head as we went round and round like cars in an underground parking garage.

Even if I didn't see Denny, I would have known I was running in the right direction by the people sprawled on the floor in his wake. I had to do my high hurdler imitation, leaping over falling bodies, my gun pointing in the air as I whizzed by.

He was waiting for me as I came around the last turn. He was down on one knee in the classic shooter's position, and the .38 spat out a bullet with my name on it. I dived to the floor and rolled as the shot whizzed past my ear, coming up with my gun in my hand and squeezing off a couple of rounds.

O'Keefe screamed and spun. One of my bullets had hit him in the shoulder. His .38 went flying into the air. At the sound of the gunshots, everyone in the corridor hit the floor. A woman screamed and an elderly man kneeled and crossed himself.

As counterpoint to the action, a group on the stage of the Forum was singing "Give Peace a Chance."

He rolled on the floor toward a crouching gray-haired dowager whose mouth and eyes were open wide with fright. I leveled the gun for a shot but had to hold my fire as a heavyset man stood up in front of me. I shoved him out of the way, but O'Keefe had pulled a switchblade from his pocket and had the blade against the woman's throat. He pulled her to her feet, keeping his back against the wall.

"Drop your gun Resnick, or the old lady's head comes off," he said threateningly. The woman moaned, too frightened to speak.

The exit door opened and Lieutenant McCoy came into the corridor on Denny's left. He spread his feet and took aim at O'Keefe.

"You too, mister. Drop your gun!" Denny said, flattening himself even more against the wall.

McCoy took in the situation. It was an old-fashioned Mexican standoff. I was fifteen feet to O'Keefe's right, my gun leveled at him. Denny stood pressed against the wall, his right hand curled around the woman's throat and the blade pressed just under her chin. McCoy stood on Denny's left, his gun aimed at O'Keefe's head. Tiny spots of blood dripped to the floor from the shoulder wound where I had winged him.

"What gives, Slots?" MeCoy called out.

"His name's O'Keefe. He wanted to be the new Sirhan Sirhan and take a pop at the vice president."

"Shut up, Resnick!" Denny screamed. "This is the last time I'm telling you two assholes to drop your guns, unless you want to see Grandma get sliced."

"Everybody get out of this area!" MeCoy yelled. "This is police business!"

There were six people on the floor between me and O'Keefe. They got to their feet and quickly ran behind me to safety.

"Put the knife away, Denny. Let me get a doctor to look at your arm," I said.

"I'll worry about my arm, okay Resnick?"

"Come on, Denny. You're not going anywhere. Throw it in before you get hurt."

"Don't worry, pal. There's a cool million bucks waiting for me downstairs. You guys aren't going to take me. I've got too much to lose."

He pushed the woman down on the floor and yanked her head back, exposing her throat. "It's now or never for the both of you! Toss your guns away or watch the blood pour!" he said angrily, sneering at me and MeCoy. "You first, copper! *Drop it!*"

MeCoy's gun flipped from his hand.

"Now you, wiseass," O'Keefe snarled.

I let the special fall out in front of me.

He dragged the crying woman down the hall in MeCoy's direction, where the exit was. He could have kept going to the door and made it to the staircase; instead, as he passed MeCoy, he pushed the woman into the lieutenant.

Somehow I knew what he was going to do. I knew it by the vicious feral look in his eye; I knew it from having dealt with twisted punks like O'Keefe all my life.

As MeCoy struggled to keep the old woman from losing her balance, O'Keefe pounced on the lieutenant's gun. He could have pocketed it and kept on going down the stairs, but I knew he wouldn't. I dived to where my gun lay on the floor as O'Keefe whirled and took two shots at me. That gave MeCoy a chance to jump him, but he was too slow.

O'Keefe stepped back and kneed MeCoy in the groin. He fell like a sack of potatoes and that gave O'Keefe the opportunity to kick him savagely in the ribs. MeCoy fell still, and O'Keefe crouched next to him. I saw him place the barrel of his gun to MeCoy's temple just as I squeezed off a round. The force of my bullet seemed to lift him into the air; It was as if a giant invisible hand had swatted him to the side. He looked at me with mild surprise and then he smiled, drooling blood. He lifted MeCoy's gun with great effort, as if it weighed a hundred pounds. I wasn't going to give him the chance to fire. I hit him twice, the bullets exiting right through his back. His arms and legs twitched convulsively and he fell face forward, dead.

I was aware of people screaming behind me as I rushed over to MeCoy. He groaned in pain as I helped him sit up.

"You okay?" I asked.

"Yeah," he grimaced. "If you hadn't plugged him, I was gone." He closed his eyes and took a deep breath. "I think he broke a rib."

I stepped over to O'Keefe and turned him over. There were red splotches of blood and small craters where the bullets had penetrated his shirt.

I reached into his pocket and pulled out a sheaf of papers. They were so-called letters of explanation, with some mumbo jumbo about the Union of the Liberators of the Working Class having found the vice president guilty of high crimes against humanity. The flyers purported to explain why it was necessary that his execution be carried out to begin the revolution that would ultimately make every man free and prosperous. Nothing like killing someone in the name of peace and freedom.

I reached into his jacket pocket and felt a set of keys and a small piece of cardboard. I knew what it was without looking, and I pocketed the cardboard and the keys without MeCoy seeing me.

MeCoy moved over to my side. He was white, but at least he was standing. "What're those flyers?" he wanted to know.

I reached up and handed them to him. He read them without saying a word.

"I got a tip from someone that a radical organization would take a shot at the vice president. I guess he would have tried it, too, if you hadn't been around to stop him, Resnick."

Just then Sloan and Tanya came running up to us. "My, God!" Sloan said.

"It's Dennis! Slots, what happened?" Tanya asked me, clutching her chest.

"Dennis was your kidnapper," I told her. "It was him and another guy. He's the one that picked up the money."

"I can't believe it," Tanya said, shaking her head.

"Well, you couldn't know. They were hoods, and you told me they always talked to you with that helium to change their voices," Sloan said to comfort her.

"What the hell is all this about a kidnapping?" MeCoy wanted to know.

"Tanya was snatched the day before yesterday. The ULWC demanded a million bucks in ransom. Sloan arranged for the money, and I dropped it off. This creep was the one who picked it up. He was bragging about a big event that would put the ULWC on the map and I figured out that it must have had something to do with the vice president's visit to the rally."

"Thank God he's on his way back to Washington," Tanya said, holding on to Sloan's arm.

"Why doesn't the FBI find the rest of these ULWC bastards," Sloan steamed.

Two cops in uniform who looked like the same team MeCoy had had with him in Wackley's apartment came running toward the lieutenant. "Are you okay, sir?" the baby-faced rookie asked.

"Yeah, I want you to take care of the stiff here, and block off all access to this area. Jerry, you ferry Mr. Sloan, Mrs. Pinto, and Resnick down to the station house, where we can sort everything out."

"Can't it wait until after the rally? It's just another hour," Sloan asked.

MeCoy shook his head. "You've been keeping the police out of things for too long. There's at least one other ULWC person still running loose, and there's also a million in cash that's not accounted for. Let's all put our heads together at the station house and see if we can't do a little explaining and a little figuring."

• •

22

I t made you think. Under the six-foot floures-
cents, a long cigarette-burned oak table filled up
the center of the room. Behind it was a window
stippled with wire mesh, giving a view of the
street outside, which was double- and triple-parked
with blue and white police cars, a handful of unmarked Furys, and a Chevy Citation. There were a
couple of desks manned by civilian employees, and
they were typing on manual typewriters and speaking into rotary phones. In the age of the Wang and
fiber optic communication, people in police stations
still sweated in tilt-back swivel chairs, making du-
plicates and triplicates of forms that could have
been processed in half the time if the people at the
top had ever heard the name Xerox.

MeCoy called me into his office and motioned for
me to take a chair across from his desk.

"I could call in a stenographer to take down your
statement, but that can wait until we get some pre-
liminaries out of the way. I guess you know the routine better than me, anyway." He placed both hands

on the desk and pushed himself away, sinking lower in his chair. Judging by the beads of sweat on his brow, the rib was giving him a lot of pain. "Why don't you pick it up from the day you were in here last. Alex Tucker was blown away and you and me had that chat—"

"Is that a piece of pop art or does the thing really make coffee?" I nodded to a Mr. Coffee sitting on the window ledge behind MeCoy's ear.

He nodded and pulled a white plastic cup from the desk and tossed it over to me. "Help yourself. I got sugar here somewhere," he said. "You have to take powdered milk, though. We used to buy cartons of milk but it was always the same guy who bought it—namely me."

"I take it straight," I told him.

"Fine. Now give it to *me* straight."

I told him everything I could about the case, leaving out the keys and the stub I took from Denny's body. MeCoy was a good listener, nodding in the right places, grunting, shaking his head in disgust when the narrative called for it.

When I finished, he pulled out a pack of Carltons and offered me a smoke. I shook him off and finished the last drop of the coffee.

"Here's how I see it," he said. "Wackley and O'Keefe were part of this Workers Liberation group. They had infiltrated Command Pictures to get the goods on Ned Pinto. Maybe they figured they could spread the word at the right time about Pinto and his child molestations."

"What about Noolan?"

"Noolan really isn't in the group. I see Noolan as being a wacko, and they figured on using him. Maybe they got someone to goad him on. They riled him up about that Agent Orange stuff, made it easy for him to get a gun, paid for his cross-country trip to nail Pinto. It wasn't enough to discredit the big slob, they figured they had to do away with him before the rally. Maybe they figured that the rally was going to cause big changes in the system, bring back Joe McCarthy days." He poked the air with his cigarette for emphasis. "Now Noolan messes up a couple of times and they're worried. They got to do something. Maybe the big poobah in Moscow is telling them to make something happen. O'Keefe puts on a blond wig and blows Pinto away. That should do it! No more Pinto, no more rally. Tommy Noolan takes the rap, and they're clear."

"Then I come along."

"Right. Now they're scared shitless that you're going to prove that Tommy couldn't have done it. They pick you up to put a scare into you, but it doesn't stick. O'Keefe goes back and rigs your car."

I picked it up. "Could it be that Wackley was turned off to the whole deal? He had something going with Arlene Diamond, and the love affair with O'Keefe was wearing thin. Maybe he had a change of heart when Tucker got killed. O'Keefe said he was going to go to the cops and that's why he decided to shut him up permanently."

McCoy nodded. "It doesn't take much with these fags," he said. "They can be vicious, when they get jealous, there's nothing they won't do. Christ, you know what I'm talking about."

"What about Tanya's kidnapping?"

"Hey, that doesn't surprise me. These people aren't playing with fifty-two, Resnick. First, they don't want any publicity, and then they want to kill the number-two man in the world. They had a change of heart, that's all. When they couldn't stop Tanya from calling off the rally, they figured they'd use it to capitalize on. They make a million bucks and have their name splashed all over the papers. O'Keefe was going to be paid well and sent away for a long vacation."

"He was going to the Virgin Islands."

"See? What'd I tell you," MeCoy said smugly.

"Maybe," I said without conviction.

MeCoy looked at me, tilting his head. "How come I'm getting the feeling that I'm not making a sale here?"

I shrugged. "I don't know. There are just a lot of little things that still bother me."

"Such as?"

"Did you ever get a look at Tommy Noolan?"

"Yeah. What about him?"

"How did Sloan and Boddiker mistake O'Keefe for Noolan? Maybe they're close in height, and maybe O'Keefe wore a blond wig, but *shit*, MeCoy! Noolan looks like a blade of grass and O'Keefe is built like a tree. Maybe I can see Sloan screwing up: he's a civilian and he panicked. But Boddiker?"

"He wasn't sitting next to Pinto, Slots. From his corner of the limo he might not have gotten too good a look."

"Yeah, I guess. That's what I thought at first. . . ."

"What else?" MeCoy asked.

"I don't see Wackley and Denny putting in all those years with Pinto in order to infiltrate the studio. From what everyone says, they had enough on Pinto to hang him. Why hold back if they were out to get him? Why not cut him down early, before his right-wing ideas got a chance to flourish?"

MeCoy shrugged. "Maybe they thought they could convert him."

"I also want to know about the third person in the room with Tanya and O'Keefe—that would be the guy who held the camera and helped O'Keefe with the kidnapping."

"That was the guy who called in the tip to me. They obviously thought Denny had done the job and they wanted the credit."

"Yeah. He's a loose end that I'd like to tie up," I said thoughtfully.

"I think I'll stick with my story, Slots. I really think—"

I didn't get a chance to hear what MeCoy really thought. There was a tap on the door and before MeCoy could say come in, Ackerman strode in, slamming the door behind him. "I want the book thrown at this slime, John. I want to bury this weasel," Ackerman said.

"Take it easy, Mr. Ackerman. I don't know that Resnick has done anything," MeCoy said.

"Then find something!" Ackerman insisted.

"I don't run an investigation like that!" MeCoy snapped.

"You don't get it, do you, John? This guy just wants to make all of us look bad. If you don't do the right thing, maybe you're not the man for the job. Maybe we need someone else, someone who understands what it's all about."

"Why don't you take a hike," MeCoy told him.

"What did you say?" Ackerman's eyes narrowed.

"I said, go take a hike. If that isn't clear enough for you, I'll kick you out of my fuckin' office!"

"When I get finished with you, mister, you'll wish you were never born," Ackerman warned. "I'm on my way to see the commissioner."

"The commissioner can do what the hell he pleases. Right now I'm on this case, and if your fat ass isn't out of here in two seconds, I'm arresting you for obstruction of justice."

Ackerman gave us both a parting dagger stare and stormed out.

"Thanks," I said.

"No thanks necessary. It felt too damn good."

• •

23

I was waiting for Sloan and Tanya in front of the station house. I had given a bare-bones statement to the stenographer, and they had followed suit.

As they stepped out, I called them over and flagged down a cab.

"What's going on, Slots?" Sloan asked.

"Take a look at this." I handed him the cardboard stub.

"It's a receipt from a parking garage," Tanya said.

"Right. I got it out of Denny's coat pocket."

Sloan shrugged. "So?"

"Get in and I'll explain."

I held the door of the cab open and joined them inside. I gave the driver the address on the parking garage receipt. It was a garage near the Garden. I had held it back from McCoy because I might have been totally off base, and I still had a responsibility to Sloan and Tanya, who were technically my clients.

"Denny planned on assassinating the vice president and leaving the country. He had to have a place to stash the money he was taking with him. It had to be accessible and it had to be in whatever he was going to use to make a fast getaway during all the excitement."

"The trunk of his car?" Sloan asked.

"Maybe," I told him. "It's worth a look."

It took us twenty minutes to get crosstown from the police station. Bert and Tanya talked about the rally. It had gone off well, and there was to be a follow-up at the Meadowlands in a week.

There was another undercurrent that I couldn't put my finger on. It had something to do with the money, something to do with a million bucks which was tax free, and for all intents and purposes, free and clear to the people who found it. Maybe that's what Sloan was thinking. Tanya, I'm sure, was figuring on how many more anti-Commie events she could plan. And I was thinking about Tahiti.

It was an underground garage with one wall filled with different-colored signs, each giving a different rate for different days, months, years, leap years . . . I never could figure out which applied to my car. Whenever I parked in one of these garages, I'd hand the attendant a twenty and stare over at the rates as if I knew what the hell I was looking at.

This one had a wood and glass shack down the steep ramp. I walked in, followed by Sloan and Tanya. The attendant was a wizened black man who looked at the ticket, punched it, and asked me for sixteen dollars. Tanya and Sloan didn't move a muscle, so I paid the man.

"You have to pick that one out yerself, boss," the man said. "Fellow who parked it wouldn't leave no key. He wanted a spot far away from all the other cars and he wouldn't leave me no key. He said he wanted to get outta here in a hurry."

"Is that right?"

"Yeah, thass right. I tole him we don't let no cars park here without the key but he laid a fifty on me and I said okay." He laughed.

"If he gave you fifty, how come you charged me another sixteen?"

"The fifty was for me and the special service I give him; the sixteen goes to the boss."

"Where is it?" Sloan wanted to know.

"All the way in the back. You'll see another opening big enough for three cars. It's all the way back there. S'cuse me." He took a ticket from a yuppie couple.

The three of us followed his directions and wound up in a deserted part of the underground lot.

"There it is." Sloan pointed to a plain brown Cutlass. The license plate said CMD3.

"It's a studio car, huh?" I said.

"Sure. Denny never had two nickels to rub together. He always drove one of the studio cars. We all used studio cars," Sloan told me.

I took out the keys and picked out the one for the trunk. Tanya and Sloan stood behind me. I put the key in and turned the lock. They were there, all right: two Samsonite bags containing a million bucks.

"It's all there," Tanya said. "One million beautiful dollars."

"Let's make sure," I told them.

I lifted up the cover and looked over a solid sea of green hundred-dollar bills.

"Beautiful!" Sloan said. "Now with Tanya safe, I really can enjoy it."

I lifted up one of the packs and rifled it. The balloon burst. There was a hundred-dollar bill on the top; under that was cut-up newspaper.

"What the hell!" Sloan whined. "What the hell is going on?"

"It was switched," I told him.

"Switched? By whom?" Tanya asked, the disappointment all over her face.

I shrugged. "O'Keefe, his partner, the ULWC hierarchy. Who knows?" I checked out the other case; it was the same. "Well, it's not a total loss," I told them. "There's ten grand, and that covers my fee."

Just then Tanya's watch alarm went off. It was five-thirty already, time for her vitamins. She reached over and shut it by pressing one of the buttons.

A little alarm went off in my head. Something was there trying to get out. I thought about the tape, I thought about Alain . . . and then I knew.

"You'll need a glass of water," I said. "Get in the car and we'll drive out of here."

"No, thanks. I feel like walking. You and Bert go on; I'll see you later at the hotel. It's been a long day, and I want to unwind."

Sloan opened the door and slipped behind the wheel. "Come on, Slots," he said. "Let's go."

"I don't want to leave Tanya. Get in the car," I said affably.

"Don't worry about me." She smiled. "I'm a big girl, I'm used to looking after myself."

"Hey, if you two want to hang around, that's fine. I want to get back and take a shower. Give me the keys, Slots," Sloan said reaching out the window.

"No. Tanya is going to drive us."

She looked at me and her brows came together. "Are you being stupid, or something? I said I'd rather walk!"

"Come on Slots, you heard her. Let's get out of here. The damn carbon monoxide is giving me a headache."

Tanya turned and started walking away from the car. I ran a few steps and whirled her around. I pulled my gun out of the holster and put it to her head. "Mr. Slots Resnick requests the pleasure of your company—in the car!" I told her through clenched teeth.

Tanya's stare was unbridled hate.

"Have you gone nuts?" Sloan wanted to know. He jumped out of the car.

I waved the gun at him. "Get back inside," I snarled. "Move it!"

Sloan looked at me as if I had lost my marbles, but he got back in the car and sat in the passenger seat. I opened the front for Tanya and pushed her behind the wheel. I opened the back door and got in, sitting directly behind her.

"Son-of-a-bitch *bastard*," she cursed under her breath.

I kept the gun at her head as I reached over and put the key in the ignition.

Sloan stared at Tanya, but she didn't look back at him. "Tanya, what's going on?" he asked softly.

"Start the car, Tanya." I commanded.

"Drop dead!"

"Resnick, what is this? What's going on?"

"Go on and tell him, Tanya."

"Go to hell, bastard!"

"It looks like your lady friend doesn't want to drive, Bert. She didn't mind if we drove away, but she'd rather walk."

I saw Bert stiffen as it finally hit him. "No!" He jumped out of the car and lifted the hood. He stood there, not moving.

I pulled Tanya out and dragged her to the front of the car. Bert was frozen, looking at the red package of explosives that was connected to the ignition wires.

"My, God," he whispered. "Why, Tanya? *Why?*"

"Shut up, Bert!"

"You would have let me die. *You would have killed me.* I thought you loved me."

"Don't you get it yet, Sloan? Tanya loves only the

Cause. You're just a soldier. Your death, Ned's death, O'Keefe and Wackley—everything for the Cause."

"That's right, Resnick! People, individual people, mean nothing!"

"You little bitch!" Sloan screamed. "I loved you! I would have done anything for you."

"You're a fool!" she snapped. "You're a weak, sniveling fool!"

"Weak? Why? Because I didn't share your lust for murder? Because I didn't want to kill O'Keefe?"

"Shut up!"

"That was the deal, Bert. She didn't want to let Denny go. She couldn't part with the money, and she wanted to be sure that Denny could never black-mail her. That's why she rigged the car. She learned all the tricks from Bill and Denny, maybe while they were out jogging in the mornings. 'Tell me, Denny, just how do you set an explosive in a car?' Poor O'Keefe never realized it might be used against him one day."

"But why me?" Sloan asked, looking straight at Tanya. "I did everything you wanted. I went along with everything."

"Because she never could fully trust you, Bert. You knew that the ULWC was just a phony front to throw everyone off. You knew that Denny didn't kill Ned. You knew that the whole scheme was cooked up to throw suspicion away from Ned's real killer— Tanya."

"Damn you, Resnick!"

"I knew Boddiker wouldn't have identified O'Keefe as Noolan. O'Keefe was too broad, and Bod-diker wasn't that far away, so he would spot the dif-ference. Tanya, you're just about Noolan's size and weight, your hair is the same color, and in a vest, speeding by on the bike, I can understand his con-fusion, especially with Sloan swearing up and down that it was Noolan."

Sloan leaned against the car and cradled his head in his hands. "What's going to happen to me now, Slots?" he asked.

In a small way, I felt sorry for the sap. He wasn't unlike a million other guys, falling head over heels for a woman and then getting the shaft. The truth of it, though, was that if Tanya had played it straight with Sloan, they would have gotten away with everything.

"The way I look at it Bert, you're ahead of the game. It wouldn't have been too long before she felt you were standing in her way, just like Ned, or Denny. She would have found a way to murder you, and then Arlene too. Little Tanya always wants it all to herself."

"And why not!" Her eyes flashed. "I'm smarter, and more ruthless. I know what has to be done, and I make it happen. Ned would have ruined everything with his taste for children," she spat out. "He never truly understood how symbolic he had become to the world," she said in a much softer tone, her eyes glazing over with the fanaticism of do-gooders everywhere. "When Noolan took a shot at Ned back in Malibu, my reflex reaction was to save him. But that started my mind working, and I realized that had I not pushed him off the lounge, I could wield the power to further the cause. I wouldn't make that mistake again. . . . In fact, I had to make it happen!"

"What about Bert?"

"Weak. He trusted people. He thought he could trust his friend O'Keefe. 'Give him a million dollars and he won't ask for more.' I couldn't live with that threat hanging over my head, and I knew Bert wasn't man enough to kill him. He wasn't man enough to kill Ned. I had to do it. I had to do everything."

"Does that include Wackley? You found out about

Bill and Arlene and you goaded O'Keefe into killing Wackley?"

"Yes. Bill was getting cold feet. He knew Denny and I put the plastic explosives in your car. He got scared and wanted to back out."

I could visualize her peering over Denny's shoulder as they set up the bomb in my Porsche. Denny and his apprentice, Tanya, working on a little project that cost Tucker his life.

"You know what I think, Bert? I think you could walk away from this with light time. You helped in the phony kidnapping and took the tape of Tanya. That's no big deal. You lied in identifying Noolan, but the jury might fall for a love story. All you have to do is turn state's evidence and tell all you know about the Black Widow here."

Tanya laughed. "Let's stop this charade. No one is going to do anything."

"Really?"

"Really! Don't forget that I have the rest of the million. That's nine hundred and ninety thousand dollars that is unmarked and untraceable."

"And you propose. . . ?"

"I propose that the money is yours, Slots. You walk away with a million dollars, and no one is the wiser. The world goes on looking for the ULWC, which fades from sight forever."

"What happens to me?" Sloan asked.

"I buy you out. You walk away a multimillionaire. If I go to prison, all the company assets will be tied up in court for twenty years. If you get out of jail in five years, you won't see a penny for more than a decade."

Sloan thought it over. "She might be right, Slots."

"You think so?"

"What the hell's the difference? This whole situation stinks. At least we can get something out of it," Sloan reasoned.

"Sorry. I'd rather be poor but happy," I told them.

"You can't be serious!" Tanya said.

"Think about what you're doing," Sloan told me.

"Oh, I know what I'm doing. I'm going to live the rest of my life without having to wonder when Tanya is going to decide to roll a hand grenade under my bed. The ten grand you folks owe me, on top of the six thousand received and Carol Simmon's fifty, will do me just fine for a while."

Tanya stared at me and shook her head. "You *are* crazy."

"Maybe, but I have the gun, and for now that's what counts, isn't it?"

24

It was lunchtime, and we were having a bite before walking down for the ceremony. Sherry was playing with her cheeseburger and looking at me. "I'll never figure you out," she said finally.

She had just read the newspaper account of the solving of the Pinto murder. I was mentioned, but only as a brief footnote: "Former police official Mickey "Slots" Resnick aided police in the capture of Tanya Pinto and Bert Sloan."

"What do you mean? You did the whole thing?" she said.

"It's not important," I told her.

"But if you got publicity on this, you'd get more cases. You're so damn smart, you could be a millionaire."

"Sometimes you don't have to be smart to be a millionaire. You just have to look the other way. The rest of the money was recovered from Tanya's car. She hadn't had the time to hide it."

Sherry thought about what I had said. "I wonder what I would have done."

"You would have done the same thing," I said.

"You think I have so much integrity, huh?"

"Nah. You'd be afraid of Tanya, too."

She stared at me, trying to see if I would smile. I kept a straight face. "That wasn't it, was it?" she asked.

"You'll never know," I told her.

"Slots Resnick! I hate you!"

"Then you don't get this." I pulled the envelope out of my pocket and laid it on the table. "It's ten thousand dollars. I've been looking for a good financial adviser and I guess I'll have to keep looking."

"Oh no, you don't!" She grabbed the envelope. "This is going to be our nest egg. That is, if you ever have the desire to nest," she added quickly.

I smiled at her and we shared the warmth of the moment. I took her hand and slowly kissed her fingers, looking directly into her eyes.

"Slots, there's something that I don't understand."

"Ze ways of love, my sweet?" I said in my best Alain Gellet.

"How did you know it was Tanya who rigged the car?"

"Oh, I knew it was one of them. It was a company car, so they both had access to the keys. When I saw the money had been switched and not taken outright, it was obvious that they wanted to fool Denny for a little while at least. He was to think the money was safe and then start the car. They obviously weren't concerned that Denny would come back at them, because Denny was to be murdered."

"But what made you suspect Tanya?"

"Her watch alarm."

"What?"

"Remember the tape of her being kidnapped? Alain told me about a watch alarm. It went off at five-thirty. That was when Tanya's watch was set to go off."

"So?"

"So, my sweet, Tanya's hands were supposed to be tied to the arms of the chair she was in. How could the alarm stop if her hands were tied to the arms of the chair? She had to have at least one hand free to press the button to stop the alarm. Otherwise it would have continued for twenty seconds."

"So then—"

"So then I knew that she was in on everything. From then on, it all fell into place."

"But why did she cook up this whole scheme? She had money, beauty, position. Why?"

"That, my love, I don't think anyone will ever completely understand. Who knows what deprivations she may have been subjected to behind the Iron Curtain, but she fought like hell to escape from there and become a part of the Free World. She made no bones about setting her cap for Ned Pinto and molding him into a symbol for freedom. I guess her passion for a totally free world became as much a right-wing obsession for her as fanaticism others associate with left-wing groups. Which only goes to prove that too much of anything can really make you crazy!"

Sherry was with me on the steps of the courthouse in Foley Square. We watched a beaming Ackerman reading a proclamation from the mayor congratulating the police department and in particular, Detective Lieutenant John McCoy, for his fine work in solving the Ned Pinto murder.

McCoy shook hands with the mayor's representative and the nervously smiling Commissioner Vargas and made a little speech. He said he was just doing his job and he was glad things came out the right way. He said he had gotten lots of help in the case from his street contacts, and he looked directly at me. Before I left he caught my eye and touched the brim of his hat in salute.

I watched the flashbulbs pop and I thought how Ackerman must be wincing inside.

I felt good, real good. Chalk up a home run for Resnick!